McAuffe's Arctic

By
LR Guffey

Order this book online at www.trafford.com
or email orders@trafford.com

Most Trafford titles are also available at major online book retailers.

Note for Librarians: A cataloguing record for this book is available from Library
and Archives Canada at www.collectionscanada.ca/amicus/index-e.html

Printed in Victoria, BC, Canada.

ISBN: 9781-4269-034-1-0

*Our mission is to efficiently provide the world's finest, most comprehensive
book publishing service, enabling every author to experience success.
To find out how to publish your book, your way, and have it available
worldwide, visit us online at www.trafford.com*

 www.trafford.com

North America & international
toll-free: 1 888 232 4444 (USA & Canada)
phone: 250 383 6864 ♦ fax: 812 355 4082

Contents

Chapter 1

Dreams

It was cold when dad disappeared, much like tonight. My mind wanders in and out, flying one minute and lost in thought the next. I've flown this route since I was a boy and thoughts wander back to the day I landed for the first time on my make shift strip, next to the cabin. The look on dads face told volumes. I was either going to get the likkin of my life or have one proud dad.

That was then, this is now and I better shake my head a few more times or its down I go. A little tap on the fuel gauge and all is well, this time. Plenty of fuel to get me there. I hope that I am right, thinking that I have a full barrel of fuel next to the strip.

There she is, I can just make out the strip as it ends thirty feet from the cabin door. Dam its getting dark. It's either my old eye sight or I misjudged when I left. Don't matter none. I've done this a thousand times. Bank to the left, one last look and throttle back. She settles like a dead duck tonight. The air is heavy. The ski's touch down with a loud scrape on ice crusted snow, bringing me fully awake. Slower, slower, come on old girl, slower, ah, just right. Swing around, point her down the strip and cut the engine. Out the door, grab the wrench out of my coveralls and get to work. I have to drain the oil while it's hot or it will be awful hard to start, even with a heated tent over her engine. I take the bucket of rapidly cooling oil to the cabin and scrape the frost off the thermometer. Looks like about 56 below, amazing, same temperature as dad said it was when he went to look for mom. I go in the door, hitting it with my right shoulder. It sticks just enough to throw me off balance, the bucket of oil flies in the air, as I make a twirl and catch it. At least I catch most of it. The rest gives a soft quiet splash on the old table. Never mind that now, got to get the stove lit. I always leave enough kindling for just an occasion as tonight. I wad up some old newspaper, stuff in the kindling and pull out a match.

One strike and the smallest of a flicker of fire. It promptly goes out. Another match, the same results. Then another, then another. Now its time to get my self together. I stop, take in a cold breath of air, take a piece of kindling like dad taught me. I frizz up the end a little with my knife and place it over the paper. One more match. It's too dark to see now and I can't afford to take any more time looking for more matches. I strike the match and the paper flickers. Just a little at first, as I watch one small piece of the frizzed kindling catch. Very intently I watch as slowly the fire catches the next piece. Smoke starts to bellow out of the stove. Forgot to open the damper. The fire slowly roars to life as I warm my fingers enough to light the kerosene lamp. Dam its cold in here! Of course, I forgot to shut the dam door.

My wife always worries when I come up here alone. She says that my memory is not what it used to be. Well perhaps she is right but I'll tell you what, I recall every story that I learned as a youngster.

That's one thing I can still do, tell stories. Runs in the blood as the folks always said. Tales of old, tales of far off places. There are tales of kings, commoners, wars, fights, gold, the list goes on and on.

As the cabin warms up, I feel better. Coming up here is always the greatest pleasure of my life. Well perhaps not the greatest. My wife, the boys, and my daughter Ladonna. Now there is a girl that takes after her grand mother. Dorthy would be proud of her. I don't know who I take after. Both her and Noah I would expect. I better cook up some grub. We have been coming here for years and always keep the place well stocked. The stove is chugging now as I put a big pot of snow on to melt for coffee.

This is the life. No town for me. Dad always stayed away from town as much as possible. Our flying service forced us to live most of our life in Fairbanks. Not Noah and Dorthy. They lived in the bush all their lives. I thaw a good moose steak in the skillet and set back with a real cup of coffee.

The stove feels good, chair tilted back and with my feet propped up, my mind once again wanders. As the steak sizzles my thoughts go to Dorthy. We still wonder where she is. It's been many years since she disappeared but one still wonders what happened. People have said that Noah committed suicide. Not to our face but those little comments and looks when the subject comes up, or there is nothing else to talk about. Knowing what I know about the people of old and their customs, I figure dad just went out and that was it. He knew what he was doing, at least that is what I keep telling my self. Dad put every thing together, setting on the table for me to find. I recall as though it was yesterday. One beautiful knife that Charlie Two Bears gave him, One velvet bag with a gold coin. It was dated 1322 and had a picture of a king on it. There was also gold dust, flakes and nuggets. In fact the gold alone was enough to put a down payment on a new Cessna and still have enough to save for the kids. The box also contained a very large nugget in a deer skin bag as well as an old pocket watch that belonged to my great grand father John McAuffe. Speaking of great, great God Almighty, the smoke from the steak is getting thick.

As I try to chew the steak, I tell my self that it's the best I have ever had. That's not the truth, but I was wandering in my thoughts and plum forgot it. Any way the fire needs to be stoked for the night. As I look around the cabin, fond memories come flooding back. The old tin coffee pot spouts steam, the aroma fills the air and I can't resist one last cup. I'll most likely regret it in the middle of the night. Cup in hand I watch the frost slowly fade from the walls. The loft where I slept as a boy invites me.

Sleep came fairly fast last night, even after the second cup. Dreams of old filled my head. Last night's fire still had a few coals left as I danced out the door for my morning call. Back in and stoke up the stove. Lots of work living like this. In town all we do is turn up the thermostat. I found the cache as full as we left it in October and I relish the smell of the bacon frying in the big skillet. It mixes well with the burned moose from last night. Marie would kill me if she knew that I seldom clean the pan when I am up here alone. There is no hurry to get any thing done as I am planning on a month's stay. The cabin is the only place that quiet's me so I can write. There seems to be a spirit here that I find nowhere else.

The folks were always talking about spirits. In fact they talked about them as though they were real. Mom had quite a few tales about some woman and two men that visited her. Dad figured out that it was Rachael. Rachael was an Indian woman who was married to one of my great, great, great, well I lose count, grand dads. In fact

I am named for both of them. Paul Rachael McAuffe The woman in the red blanket, the bow woman. They lived way back in the 1600's. Part of their story was told in the manuscript that dad left for me. I always looked for them when I was younger but never saw them, unless you count the time I was setting on a ridge. Way off in the distance I thought I saw them, moving slowly, three dots. I kind of shook off the notion and chalked it up to three moose. Still, wonder about it though.

Spirits or not there are still some chores that need to be done. They won't get done with me sitting on my butt. The thing about chores, is that they are just that, chores. I have enough wood stacked up to last all winter thanks to the boys. It still needs to be split and hauled into the wood box. This done, it's clean off the frost on the wings of the old Piper Cub. That plane is ancient as planes go. People in town can't understand why when I have other newer aircraft, that I still fly this one. Even after all these years I still love her. The first plane I ever owned. I've stacked up other planes but not her. She's been rebuilt from the ground up twice and I can still fly her into places that the others won't go. I sweep the frost off the wings, something I should have done last night. The wing covers are pulled out of the cabin and another cover is placed over the engine. Before I put the warm oil back in, I'll build a small fire in a pot and warm the engine. Should start as well as usual. I think about Charlie Two Bears as I go about my work. I never could call him grand dad. It never seemed right. He always seemed to be just Charlie Two Bears. The times he and I were hunting were special. Charlie Two Bears and grand ma Addie always had me down to their place at Fortuna Ledge. I more than likely spent about as much time with them as with the folks. Charlie Two Bears could hunt. Born into it, hunted all his life. He had the general store at Fortuna Ledge but there never was much business. He left that up to grand ma. From the time that I was able to shoulder a rifle, we hunted.

Charlie Two Bears was always going on about how much of a green horn my dad was. He told me that I had more sense than dad. Said that dad had spent too much time in Nome. Said that he was lucky to be alive when he met him. Funny, dad always said it was the other way around. Dad told me that he had a great time tramping along with his dogs after he left Nome. Charlie Two Bears said that dad was half dead. I think that it was just two old guys putting each other on. Any way, where was I? I've got the snow setting on the stove melting, the wood in and my belly full, as I try to recall just what I wanted to do next. Take a nap, that's what it was. Seems like I get tired more lately.

I feel better now that I have caught up on some rest. The light didn't last long. Not real daylight, but that light that sort of looks like its going to happen but doesn't. Bread is in the oven and smells great. When we lived here, mom would keep the yeast on the back of the stove going all the time. When out on the trail she carried it in a little skin pouch under her shirt. Now days I carry it in a plastic bag under my long handles. I am not much of a cook but I get by. My wife cooks better. Only been here one day and already missing her and her cooking.

Food has always been a big part of our lives. Dad's stories always talked of food. I don't know if he was elaborating or not. I can't imagine taking in the amount of food that he talked about. Makes my mouth water just thinking about it. Of course when we gather for Christmas and Thanks giving we eat till it hurts. I think they were more social than we have become.

I woke this morning and called to a little furry dog. I rushed around the cabin and checked out side. I must have been dreaming. The problem is that the dream, if it was one was so real. This little dog came to the door all frozen and I brought it in. The thing was almost dead and I couldn't figure out how it could have gotten here or survived at all in this cold.

Chapter 2

Healing Hand

I can't believe that a week has gone by. One day runs into another. My daughter has been here for two days. At the first hint of day light, she slipped her ski equipped Beaver onto the strip as smoothly as her old man would. Her anger has subsided somewhat by now. We bedded down her plane without a word, then all hell broke loose.

"What in the world are you thinking of, coming up here without a word to any of us? Where is your head? Don't you know that we worry about you?" All this before we hit the cabin door. I am some what giving you the impression that her words were tame. What she really did was let out a string of cuss words that I had no idea that she knew. She has been silent since. Occasionally I can sense that she wants to say some thing but I don't know what.

"That was a fine meal girl." More silence. " I miss all of you, especially your mother." Ladonna started to cry and I couldn't figure out why. "You haven't said a word about your mother, how is she?" After a long pause, long enough to stop her sobs, she finally spoke. "Dad don't you remember? Mom's been dead for three months." I just sat there trying to take in what she just said. "No, Ladonna she's not." "Dad your not being real. She's gone and you absolutely won't believe it." "Listen girl, she was here just yesterday." "I won't believe that dad, I have been right here. Don't you think I would know if she was here?"

She left the subject drop as we went on to other chores. I went out and re stocked the wood box, and made a visit to the cache. The air was cold enough to freeze my nostrils shut and I was hurrying to bring in the food supplies, when a woman's voice came through loud and clear. "Paul, were here with you." I listened for what seamed like a long time. I heard no more. What was happening to me?

I continued to ponder what I had heard as I went through the cabin door, with food for supper. Ladonna was at the stove scraping the skillet into the open grate of the stove. " Don't you ever clean these pans after you use them? Put that stuff down and I'll pour you a cup". I sat back with a steaming cup in hand, I looked at Ladonna. I wiped tears from my eyes, while I thought of how she resembled my mother. This young woman, the pride of my life, was up here trying to get me to believe that her mother was gone. She worked deftly as she put the skillet back on the stove and prepared supper. I offered to do it but she politely refused. "Don't like my cooking"? " It's not that dad, I just need to keep busy."

I continued to watch in amazement as I thought of this little girl grown into a woman. She has always been more like Dorthy than anyone else. From the time that she was old enough, she could not wait to go see Grand ma so she could drive her team of dogs. She had the ability. Natural born to it as Dorthy was. I used to worry about her going out by herself but no amount of scolding stopped her. I wonder where she gets her stubbornness from.

After supper and while I cleaned every thing up, I saw Ladonna looking at me with what I thought was sadness. " I heard a woman's voice today." That got her attention. "You what?" "I heard a woman's voice while I was at the cache." Ladonna rolled her eyes, as I went on. "The woman told me that they were with me." Rolling her eyes once again, all she could get out was, "Now your hearing voices." She went on. "What else did they say? That is assuming that you really did hear voices. Who are they?"

I didn't reply to her last remark. I just left it hanging, like nothing was going on. "You're coming back with me. You will come with me, and you will go see the doctor as soon as we get back!" Now what's a guy supposed to say to that, except that it isn't going to happen.

We argued back and forth for several hours, nether giving an inch. Sleep did not come quick as I tossed and turned all night. At times I could hear her doing the same in the warm loft.

I guess I finally slept and I woke with a start as I heard the engine of the Beaver bark to life. I dressed quickly and ran down to the strip, just as she gunned the throttle and lifted off. The air was clear in the pre dawn light and I watched till she disappeared.

Alone again. Somehow it's not the same. She's gone, Dorthy's gone, Noah's gone, but not my wife. She can't be. I just saw her. What about the voice?

I worked half heartedly at the few things that I had to do. Time seemed to stand still. "Paul." I hear it again. That voice. "Paul Rachael." I look around, but there is no one in the cabin except me. I am afraid to answer. "Paul we are with you. Do not fear. The stories of your people are right. We are Rachel, Paul and Simon. Your wife is safe. She sends you her love. We are her messengers. We have been with your family for many years. We are part of you."

At that, I don't know what to think. I know all the stories and I have always thought them to be just that, stories. " I can hear you but I can't see you." "Would it be better if you could see us?" "Well if I am to believe you, yes." "Paul Rachael you are a doubting Thomas."

I don't know how long I sat there but the room was getting cold. I stoked up the fire in disbelief at what I heard. I still scratched my head at the thought of what I heard and was turning supper over in the skillet, when I sensed someone behind me. As I turned, I dropped the fork on the floor.

There sat my wife, with three people that I didn't know. "Paul it's me. These are Rachael. Paul and Simon. I have been allowed to contact you and ask that you not greave for me any longer. I am happy and I want you to be happy." As I tried to absorb what was happening, I could feel the woman in the red blanket touch me. Suddenly all was well and they were gone.

I awoke to a cold cabin some time the next day. I felt like the weight of the world had been lifted off my shoulders. Now I know. There is a spirit world and we are blessed. For the first time I began to pray. Not a prayer of petition but one of thanks giving for all that I have. There is a God and I felt loved for the first time. The folks tried to teach me about the need to have something or someone to believe in. Until now I had no intention of even thinking about it.

As I worked out side, I could feel a presence, a warmth and longing to see my kids. I picked up an arm full of fire wood and as I did, I turned my head. Off in the distance were four people waving to me. Then they were gone. Almost at the same time the Beaver glided in for a landing. My elation at all that was happening was almost too much to bare. Ladonna looked out the left window as the prop swung to a stop. I was grinning from ear to ear, as all three kids made a quick exit from the aircraft.

We embraced for a long time. Long enough for the kids to say they were getting cold. I for one felt no cold. Once in side, they all threw off their parkas and started talking at once. Their common thread was the four people waving, just off the end of the strip. The second thought was one of puzzlement, that there were no tracks in the snow. I managed to get them settled down, just long enough to tell my story.

The boys thought their sister right, in what she told of my condition. Ladonna however was having second thoughts.

All through the evening as my sons took turns stoking the stove, I elaborated on the events. Ladonna kept the coffee pot full and there was a certain amount of rum gone from the medicine bottle by morning. Though the kids knew most of the family stories, there was no remembrance of Paul and Rachael except by Ladonna. I guess that is why family stories must be told over and over. In modern life everyone is too busy and can't take the time to be together and share their lives.

While we sat around the table, I told how Paul had gone to Virginia in 1667. I told of his rescue by Rachael and Simon, the village life, the bow shooting contest, the iron works and the big trip down the Ohio river, to the Mississippi. As I finished, I looked over to the old double bed in the corner to see these siblings, all adults now, curled up fast asleep. I covered them with the old bear hide robe, stoked the fire one last time and headed for the loft.

Ladonna was the first one up, had the fire roaring and as I managed to open one eye, I recalled that it was me that drank most of the rum. Ladonna took one step up the ladder and handed me the first cup of Joe for the day. The boys stirred at her voice but that was as much as they could manage. I vaguely recall these young gentlemen helping me with the rum.

I hummed, as I helped Ladonna cook breakfast. "Your chipper today dad. You're different from when I left." I replied with some remark that didn't seem to suit Ladonna. "What I mean dad, is that when I left, you were confused, very confused."

As we prepared breakfast, the boys came in, each with an arm load of wood. Dropping their load in the wood box, both said they were starving. Their sister told them that they would have to wait. Joe tried to slip behind her and grab some morsel, Ladonna smacked him on the hand with the gooey spoon, that she was using to mix biscuit dough. I continued checking on the big ham thawing in the oven.

That morning was the happiest time that I could recall. I had full memory of Marie's death. I could now accept that. More than that, it was the realization that she was happy. She had been sick for a long time. I had to watch her wither away from cancer. She had been an active woman and in the end was reduced to nothing.

We sat down to a full table. The big ham that I fixed with a glaze made from a can of pineapple, hot biscuits, about half pound of bacon and scrambled powdered eggs. Desert was for later, when an apple pie came out of the oven.

The meal was great, conversation pleasant and the boys wondered why they had come up here in the first place. They all wanted me to return to town with them but I refused. It was agreed that someone would return with supplies and in too short of time they were gone.

Chapter 3

Ladonna the Story Teller

There is no reason any more that I live in Fairbanks. The kids are all buying me out of the business. I have all the money that I will ever need and I am happy to live the quiet life. I soon settled into a routine. On occasion I put on the snow shoes and packed about twenty miles. From my camp I can hike into the lower reaches of the mountains. I took pictures of the sheep, eagles and ravens, as well as any thing else of interest. A few days of these activities and I am always ready to return to the cabin. There is no reason to take these hikes, except that it keeps my survival skills sharp.

Survival skills are the things needed when suddenly faced with unplanned events. Of these, modern society with all its modern ways is grossly lacking.

Back in the cabin I sit at the table writing. The stove at my back chugs as it always does when working well. The stove is old, having come over the trail of 98 to Dawson. It managed to show up at Fortuna Ledge, where Charlie Two Bears gave it to my father. It's a little rusty on the back side but that's ok. The heat penetrates my being on this cold night. Thinking of the fire in the old stove reminds me of the family stories. How many stories have been told setting around a fire, over the last thousand years? I wish I knew all of the tales that have been lost. The story of John and Ootah and their families are of the first I learned. Chill penetrates me as I think of John's survival, warmed only by the seal oil lamps of his rescuers.

Day light is starting earlier. Winter is on it's way out. It's been only 23 below for the last week. Far easier to take than the bitter cold of two months ago. My mood is getting more somber. I don't want to leave here but I miss everyone. I consider uncovering the old Piper and going to town.

Ladonna returned early this morning, breaking off the left ski after dropping too hard onto the strip. Not much damage but it will take a little effort to repair. We unloaded the supplies and secured the Beaver before going into the cabin for lunch. "I was beginning to think no one was coming," I said while loading the stove. Ladonna seemed happy as she started to unpack the small mountain of stuff that she brought. I unthawed another moose steak in the skillet and set her place at the table. "Scrape that skillet Dad" she chided.

"Looks like an awful lot of supplies for one man." Ladonna popped back, "what do you mean one man? I'm moving up here with you." I pored the coffee and laid out the meal for us, all the while thinking that I better not push this. Ladonna and I can get into some heated arguments and I was too happy to see her, to push the subject.

We decided to wait till morning to start the repairs of the ski. That evening we sat around playing cards without further discussion of her plan. As soon as it was light enough I went out to the Beaver and took off the damaged ski.

By the time I made it back into the cabin, breakfast was ready. Of course she had to start in on me about the crud built up inside the skillet. I let it slide this time. I was getting used to living alone and this was the first test. I jokingly replied that her mother couldn't stand my evil ways in the kitchen either. That set her off. I got the full lecture on sanitation that her mother used to give me.

By the next day I had forgotten all about the reasons I had for her not staying. I liked the cooking, the conversation and the company too much to do otherwise. The ski was easy to fix, this time. I have had them broken so bad that it was all I could do to make any thing out of them.

Ladonna had a surprise for me. She had sat out the old tin box that belonged to my dad. It was setting on the same old table as though it had never been moved. I looked at her and started to choke up. The lid gave a small squeak as I slowly and reverently opened it. It was no surprise to find one old deer skin bag, one velvet bag, one old pocket watch and a beautiful knife. As I gazed on these items, tears came to my eyes. They were much as I had left them. The gold that was collected over a life time by my father was elsewhere. On the bottom lay my dad's manuscript, much tattered with age. I moved away from the box, not being able to go on. Ladonna came over and put her arms around me, as I wept.

I had to sit down. Ladonna and I sat for a long time, coffee in hand, drinking in the silence, mixed with winters cracking trees and chugging stove. Ladonna moved to the box as I sat back and listened to her. "I was born in 1956, you were born in 1935, Grand dad Noah was born in 1900." She then went on with the dates of birth for all the ancestors. Then one by one she picked the treasured items from their resting place. " This is the pocket watch that belonged to my great- great- grand father John." She slowly picked up the velvet bag. Most of the velvet sheen worn with age. "This velvet bag belonged to Inga, my great grand mother." Slowly opening it, Ladonna fingered a coin. "This coin has a picture of a king and is dated 1322." The old knife was next. The knife was beautiful in her hand. It had a blade about 8 inches long, covered with the patina of age. The handle was hand made from moose antler. An inscription scrimshawed into the handle said. Noah McAuffe. "My grand father's knife, made by Charlie Two Bears my great grand father, husband of Addie." I sat in amazement as I listened. Never before had I even thought that the kids were listening to my stories. Ladonna went on. She gently picked up the old deer skin bag and with slim fingers pried it open. "This is the Skipping Rock." It was smooth and glistened as though it had just been picked from a stream. "Rachael, my middle name sake gave this to Paul some time in the middle 1600's." Ladonna turned the rock over and over in her hand, while going to the table. I poured her another cup and laced it with a half jigger of rum. While I put on another pot of coffee, I realized that this was going to be a long night. Ladonna seemed to be lost in thought as the light of the kerosene lamp played shadows across her beautiful face. The rock glistened as she gently laid it on the table. "I like the story of the Skipping Rock. I used to imagine all kinds of things about it when I was little. As I am older, it's hard to believe that she used gold as a play thing. It was a good name for the manuscript that grand dad wrote, Skipping Rock. It's just like the family, skipping from place to place." Ladonna talked into the night. Telling stories from the old manuscript. Lloyd and Angelene, Old John and Ootah, Ewotok of the Fish, John and Mattie and finally, was too tired to go on.

The next morning I fixed breakfast as Ladonna gently stirred. The pride in my daughter overflowed. A natural story teller. Some times we wait a lifetime to finally see in one split second, the gifts of our children. This time it was I that handed a cup up to Ladonna. With the bacon off the stove, I stirred the powdered eggs into some resemblance of scrambled eggs. Ladonna held her head as she went out the door. Perhaps I put too many half jiggers of rum in her coffee.

Chapter 4

Spirit

Time flies, the weather is getting warmer. As I do some maintenance on the Cub, I hear a loud crack. Jumping to my feet in surprise, I look toward the river. The ice is making an attempt to move out and the snow is melting faster than usual. At this rate I will have to convert the Cub to tundra tires, both of which are in Fairbanks. Ladonna has taken her Beaver down to Allakaket to visit old friends. She is not expected back for a week. It's not a problem, just thinking,

That's all I do any more is think and write. I miss Ladonna even tho we argue quite a bit. The latest rift is ongoing. I open my mouth and put my foot in it more often than I would like. All I did was ask her when she was going to get married. Seems like a reasonable question. After all this is 1989,She is in her thirties and maybe I am old fashioned. I was married at eighteen. She said, in no uncertain terms, that it is none of my business. Business or no business I miss her. I have gone through all the routine maintenance on the Cub, stocked the wood box, took an inventory of the food stocks, as well as read every thing in the place. I'm going stir crazy. It's time for some excitement.

I awake early, eat a quick bite and have the heat going under the Cub. I refill the engine with oil and find a replacement after some rummaging in the shed for that which was spilled. It's not long and I spin the prop. Several tries later she spins to life. I jump in the cabin and play with the throttle as she warms up. I've already worked the ski's loose, where they were frozen to the snow. Full throttle and its off I go.

In the air I feel better. It's been awhile and at first the controls feel strange. Mechanical equipment reacts differently in colder temperatures. A lifetime of flying and it's not long and all is well.

After twenty minutes I still don't know where I'm going. Just around and around. I spot two moose off to my left and bank to take a closer look. Dropping down on the deck I make another pass. I zoom by no more than one hundred feet over their heads. Enough of that, I return to the cabin.

I bed down the Cub and head for the door with my bucket of oil. As I look up, I jump and again spill all the oil. Setting in my path, a dog, a big one, a great snarl on its face. It's obvious that I am the intruder in it's domain. It doesn't make a move. Big, about ninety pounds, snow white, head to tail. I stand there for what seems like an hour. I finally decide to make a move. "Where the hell did you come from?" Silence, obviously, It doesn't speak my language, just a snarl. As I think about my next move, I observe the impossible. There are no tracks in last night's snow. The dog is just there, nothing around it. No visible evidence that anyone or any thing has been here but me. It snowed about an inch last night and my tracks of a few hours ago are plain to see. I set the bucket down slowly, keeping one eye on the dog and the other on the food cache. Slowly I back up, nothing happens. Feeling brave I step the ten or so yards to the cache. I look back and find the dog still in the same place, snarl evident. I quickly grab one big hunk of old caribou rump and throw it in the direction of the dog. It calmly walks over to the meat and lays down with it. One sniff and the dog gives another big snarl. Strange, Its tail has ever so slight a wag to it. First dog I have seen to snarl and wag at the same time. Should I run for the cabin door or should I sit down and study this big thing. I decide to run for the door. Once inside I look out the window. It's calmly chewing on the frozen meat.

Dog or no dog it's getting cold in here. As the fire gets built up, I go back and forth to the window. There it is, quietly gnawing on the meat. The coffee boils and I am lost for a few minutes on watching the grounds spin around in the big pot. It doesn't take much to keep me entertained. Back to the window and it's not there. Suddenly a loud scratch on the door. I crack the door open just enough to see the tail wagging rapidly. Now what do I do? Gathering all the courage or stupidly I can, I open the door and let it in.

No attack, it simply walks over to the stove and lays down, all the while with a snarl on it's face. I poor a cup and walk to the table.

Looking at the dog I realize, that is not a snarl. That's a grin. Goofiest looking grin, I've ever seen. I bust out laughing. Boy, I wanted a little excitement and I got it.

This big dog rolls onto it's back and stretched out, must be five feet, nose to tail. A female, I re estimate her weight at one hundred pounds if she is an ounce. I have to go to the stove and start supper. As I stoke up the fire one more time, the big lady comes over to me. Goofy grin and all. " You ready for supper?" I go to the shelf and get down the oat meal. " How about some oats?" She looks at me and then the moose steak I am flipping in the skillet. "No, you don't, this is mine. You just finished your treat out side." I turn my back and head for the table. A loud yowl and a crash. The steak disappears down her large mouth before the skillet hit the floor. "Burnt your nose, serves you right. Now I have to go out and get another one." I return and find the oatmeal pot is on the floor, empty.

Ladonna returned three days ago and it was love at first site. "Spirit" was the first thing out of her mouth, after I told her of our adventures. They get along famously. We sat at the table as was our usual habit after supper. Ladonna told of her visit down to Allakaket. There were several cousins and they caught up on all the gossip. One of Charlie Two Bear's sons had moved there long ago. He had a large family and has since died. I was sorry when it happened. My favorite uncle.

Ladonna is gone again. This time to Fairbanks for supplies. No loneliness this time, Spirit is almost too much company. She eats like a horse. At least she is cleaning out the older meat from the cache. It will be a good excuse to hunt. When we are outside, she chases any thing moving. In the cabin she lays quietly by the stove. Spirit has taken up residence at night behind the stove next to the wall. I still consider from time to time, where she came from. I can think of all kinds of things but then it always comes back to the lack of tracks. Ladonna has her pegged. Spirit, is what she will remain to us.

Chapter 5

Hunting and Proposal

May finds a new world. Spring came in with a bang. In fact it seemed early. The ice went out fast. The willows are out, the Ptarmigan have changed from white to a mottled color and I saw the first bear of the season. No need to worry as it was way off in the distance. Fishing is good and Spirit and I already have a good amount drying over a slow fire.

Spirit and I went out last week and found a young moose feeding on new shoots of pond grass. I didn't know how Spirit would act while hunting. There was no need for concern as she did her part well. The young moose brought in about 400 pounds of meat. Ladonna had made Spirit a new pack and she carried almost half of the moose in two trips. That has been cut into strips and Spirit and I have the last of it drying over the fire. Spirit has learned to fish. In fact she usually does better than the bears. She stands in the shallows and as soon as she spots what she wants, its one swipe and up on the bank it comes. Occasionally she will stick her head under water and get one that way. She eats her fill and its food that I don't have to feed her.

One of the boys is on his final approach and about to drop onto the strip. I always love to see an aircraft land. Like usual it's taxi up to the shop swing around and cut the engine. Joe has a passenger. Someone I have never seen before. The two jump out and before I can blink an eye Ladonna is out of the cabin and running up to this guy. One leap and she has her arms around him like a bear in a bear hug. She is happier than I can ever recall.

That was yesterday. The two of them walked off together, like no one else was around. It wasn't till last night that he was introduced. I hadn't said a word, I guess trying to get over the shock of seeing someone hugging my little girl, other than my self. While Joe and I fixed supper, Ladonna sat with her friend making goggle eyes at one another. Enough to make an old man sick. Spirit just laid in the middle of the floor taking it all in. I did notice however that this guy kept a weary eye on Spirit. I guess he thought Spirit's snarl was real. Finally Ladonna apologized for her bad manners.

"Dad this is Alnook, Al for short." I am defiantly not prepared for this. I stick out my hand only to have it half crushed with enthusiasm. "Mister McAuffe, I have heard a lot about you." " Mister McAuffe?" I stop my self after that comment. This young man at once impresses me. "There's no need to call me mister, I'm Paul."

I am amazed. Al is about six feet tall. Tall for a native. A Canadian from, Prince Charles Island. west of Baffin Island. His father a Scotsman, worked for the weather service in that area. This time it was Ladonna that poured the rum into my coffee. I could see that Al was anxious to make an impression, so the three of us listened as Al told tales of long ago.

For a few minutes I half listened to him and half thought of Old John and Ootah. His stories were strangely familiar. Not only do I think it strange that his last name is Maguffy but that he can trace it back to Colonsay. Even above that, he knows some of the stories of the family. This is too much for me. I say good night and crawl up to the loft.

I toss and turn most of the night and wake with a headache. Al, Ladonna, Joe and Spirit are gone. The stove is still hot and I cook up a good breakfast even though I am hung over. Images from the stories that Al told race through my head. I try and busy myself all day but by late afternoon start to get concerned. It's not like the kids to leave with out a note. As several more hours pass, visions of a horror pass through my mind. All through the twilight hours that pass for night in the summer, I wait. Finally about three in the morning I crank up the Cub and go looking. I fly an ever widening circle from the cabin. No one insight. I decide to make one more pass to the North. Almost to the limit of fuel, there they are below and slightly to the West of my location. I bank left and drop for a closer look. As I pass over, Spirit is in the lead with her pack more than full. Al is next in line, his pack piled high, Ladonna and Joe are not there. I circle a few times pointing to a clearing. Al gets the message and by the time I drop onto the short almost non existent strip. He and Spirit arrive.

Puffing under the load, Al informs me that Joe and Ladonna are about four miles North and setting under some willows next to the river. They had a successful hunt and managed to make a good catch of Grayling. Ladonna had sprained an ankle and was unable to walk. We agreed that Al and Spirit would return to the kids and I would take the meat back to the cabin and get more fuel. Al said that there was a good place to land about one quarter mile from Ladonna's location. He planned to hike back and carry Ladonna to it. Between the two loads of meat and fish I had about two hundred pounds of extra weight. The Cub lifted off the ground with just inches to spare. Luckily I was low on fuel. As the dwarf trees glided under the Cub I could see Al and Spirit already returning.

I landed at the cabin with fumes in the tank. After off loading the supplies I refueled and cleared the end of the strip faster than usual. I feel better now that I am back in the air and heading for the kids. I am proud of the way Al has handled the situation. Joe is not the best navigator in the field. Al is the expert in that department as I see exactly the location he described. It is short but I drop in with class. Ladonna's ankle is as big as a balloon. Al has it well protected, as we place her in the Cub. It is not too great a distance back to the cabin and we say fair well to the packers and take off.

The next day the three packers come in bushed and hungry. Ladonna lay on the lower bed with her foot elevated. Al greets Ladonna with tenderness and a few words that I can't quite hear.

It's too warm to cook in the cabin, so next to the drying racks, I have a fire going under a pot of beans. Large portions of fish fry in one skillet and a mess of bear grease and frying potatoes, are heaped in the other. Al has come out of the cabin carrying Ladonna. The guy continues to impress me with the way he treats her. After getting her situated comfortably, he comes over to me and sets down. "Coffee"? I ask him. "You bet". The pot hangs from a hook over the fire and I hold the bottom with a stick as I tilt a cup full for my guest. I offer a small shot of rum for it but Al refuses.

"Good dog" Al offers. "We used to have a lot of dogs at home but not so much any more, too modern. No one wants to feed them when they can have a new snow machine." Al talks of all the dogs he has had, than suddenly switches the subject. "I want to marry your daughter." He adds that they have known each other for a long time. They met at the University of Alaska at Fairbanks. Each were taking advance degrees. Ladonna already had a degree in wildlife management but had more interest in archeology. Al said his two degrees included native studies and wildlife management. When they met they were taking a special course in the relationships of Muskox to the Native Peoples.

I didn't need to think long or give the impression I opposed the union. "Al, I think we will all get along just fine, go ahead and ask her." "I just wanted to get your permission, Ladonna has said that you are old fashioned." "Old fashioned"? I gave a wink to Al and pored another cup. Later, as I came out of the out house, I saw Al packing Ladonna on one shoulder toward the river.

Chapter 6

Spirits First Flight

That night Ladonna and Al informed us that they were to be married later in the summer. In the meantime Al had to return to work. Ladonna flew him and her brother back to Fairbanks the next day, leaving me to process all the meat and fish. I was glad for the chores to do, as it kept my mind occupied. All in all, counting the meat that Spirit and I had, as well as the recent success, we had about 700 pounds of dried meat and sixty or seventy pounds of dried fish.

I needed a change of scenery so after checking the Cub, I loaded in supplies and Spirit, taking off at about four in the morning. Spirit seemed to enjoy flying. I was a little apprehensive at first but she just grinned. We flew South West down the Koyukuk River and stopped at Bettles for fuel. We stayed at my nephews house for the night and on the next day to Kobuk. I hit some turbulence on that leg and Spirit got air sick, puking all over the back of my neck. I was glad to land as the smell was over powering. Spirit and I camped under the wing that night. The mosquitos were bad and after some breakfast we were again in the air. I had topped off the fuel in Kobuk and must have run into some stale fuel. The engine ran sluggish all day. It never gave me too much concern and when we landed at Kiana, I drained the fuel. The lines needed to be checked and the filter changed. I always carry a small bag of spare parts and the job was done in no time. The new fuel was not aviation gas but some left over from last years supply. I was lucky enough to find some one with any at all. The Cub ran fine all day and after a stop for lunch on a long sand bar we arrived at Kotzebue. We stayed for a couple of days. None of the local dogs bothered Spirit. In fact they all shied away from her. The people stopped and stared at her all the time. No one spoke to us. I found this odd as the people are always friendly.

I was anxious to visit with some of my mothers family and we took off, heading up the coast. The weather was great, the sea calm and I relished the sight of whales as they surfaced. There are many times in this area that bad weather causes problems. We bypassed Kivalina and flew on to Point Hope.

I was invited to stay in the home of my grandmother's sister. I could have stayed about anywhere as I was welcomed with open arms. While I gazed on the face of my great aunt, I could imagine how my grand mother would have looked at this age. There were deep lines in her face. Her skin was a deep brown and had the texture of old leather. Her toothless smile told volumes. She was ancient. The little house was soon packed with relatives. As the people kept coming, I began to wonder if they were all mine. The introductions flew, I realized that they were indeed. The small crowd soon spilled out into the front of the house and a big fire of drift wood was going on the beach. I don't know where all the food came from but before long we were all eating and talking at once. I felt as though I had lived there all my life. As the old people sat around talking, the young people gathered in a circle and began a blanket toss. Higher and higher each young person was tossed in the air. Laughter abounded and I thought these people the happiest in the world. We sat around the great fire listening to tales of long ago hunts. Some of the people danced the dance that only these people knew. I was stuffed. The food rich. Seal, muk tuk, beaver tail, salmon and whale. My favorite from childhood, Eskimo ice cream, which is seal oil and blue berries.

They were especially interested in Spirit. At first they were suspicious of her snarl but soon realized that this was a happy dog. They had a great respect for her. Some of the children petted her and some little ones even crawled upon her great back. Mostly they told of the good omen of this great white dog. They said that they had seen her many times. There were some that said that she was a polar bear spirit. Some had seen her when they were hunting among the ice fields. There were many stories about her but most agreed that she always led hunters to safety.

The days were long and the nights only a memory this far North. Soon it was time to think of leaving. They begged us to stay and we did postpone for a few more days. When Spirit and I were ready to climb back into the Cub they started bringing presents.

There was a beautiful summer parka for Ladonna, Mukluks for Al and the boys, and a beaver fur winter hat for me. They were all hand made of the finest that these people had to offer. I had nothing to leave with them for their hospitality and felt bad for it. My great aunt Sarah told me to treat Spirit well, as she would save my life one day. A shiver ran up my spine at these words, there was enough native in me, to believe that she had some omen of things to come. Every one backed away as the Cub came to life. I waved and slipped down the strip and into the air. I made one circle and waved one last time. I wondered if I would ever see these people again. I swung South of the Delong Mountains and soon was heading for home along the Noatak River. The sky was clear and as usual I became lost in thought. Below, the river glistened as the sun played with the ripples on the water. Here and there an arctic fox. A great eagle flew next to me for a short distance but I was faster and soon out ran him. Occasionally I would run across a small heard of caribou. Nothing like dad and Charlie Two Bears talked about.

I long for the old days. Even when I was young, the world of the North seemed more free. As I fly along I realize that now there is a great park not too far from my home. The great fathers in the South have deemed that we need such a thing. I don't think that one in a million people in the South, will ever tramp these wild places. Why have a park. Even the area that I live in North of Wiseman is getting too crowded. The pipe line and the road to the North Slope is not too many miles from my cabin. We have always lived free. Now I have to watch for government men when I hunt for the food that we need. I suppose they would prefer that I run out to the store for Texas beef.

We head South to Shungnak for fuel. This is about my only choice. It is not too far from Kobuk, I don't need any more bad fuel. Spirit and I both need a break as we slip onto the strip. With the fuel toped off we leave at once for Bettles. I have friends there and we are welcomed. Knowing that Ladonna may already be back at the cabin, Spirit and I only spend one day resting and visiting. After many miles we arrive back home safely.

Ladonna stood at the stove as Spirit and I came thru the door. Spirit is over excited to see her and just about knocks her over. After a long hug, I throw my gear in the corner and sit at the table. " Well tell me all about it. Where all did you go?"

I went thru every detail of the long trip and embellished as much as possible with out being caught in a tall tale, "What you been up to?" Ladonna poured us a cup as we sat down to a great meal. "Well Dad the arrangements are all set. We will be married in September at the little church down on Cushman street. All I'll need is for Al to return from Banks Island on time."

Chapter 7

Wedding Plans

As the wedding approached I made plans to leave the cabin. The nights were shorter and I had to get in one more fall hunt as well as store supplies. I looked forward to the wedding. Not only that but to having some time to spend with the priest. My wife had been a regular part of the Catholic Community for all these years but I had not. All the events with the visions and voices as well as Spirit's arrival left me in deep thought a great deal of the time. I needed some one to talk to.

Spirit and I managed to get in the last of the meat supply just in time. I closed up the cabin and Spirit hopped into the back of the Cub. We were off to town.

We flew for a few miles before picking up the pipe line. I was lost in thought again as I recalled all the virgin territory that used to be below me. The pipe line is like a big scar on the land. The haul road is not any better. There is nothing I can do about it. We fly over the Yukon River, with a short stop at Livengood to see old friends and add fuel, then on to Fairbanks.

I had almost forgotten what it is like to come home. I picked up enough property in the old days to have my own strip. As I approached the strip the familiar buildings came into view. The large hanger about one hundred feet from the house and the out buildings behind the hanger. The kids greeted me with their usual chatter and soon the Cub was nestled in her own spot in the hanger.

The house seemed strangely empty as I entered. I flashed back over the years, recalling all the times that my wife had greeted me. That emptiness vanished abruptly as I was greeted by some of Ladonna's friends. Cheryl, Sue, Kathy, Brenda, and Kate. The kitchen was a buzz. The bar was set up on the counter and all sorts of snacks were laid out. Some one checked the oven as Ladonna introduced me to her girl friends. My son Dave came in with Spirit. It was humorous to watch the young men step back at the site of Spirit's snarl. Tail wagging, she was as happy as a lark. It didn't take long for the room to warm to her. Spirit soon learned that she could go from person to person and beg morsels that she soon learned to like.

As the final preparations for the wedding took place, the boys and I worked in the hanger. The first order of business was to take out and replace my tired old engine. It actually was the third engine for the old plane. The boys had a surprise for me, as they brought out a brand new, one hundred horse Lycoming flat four engine. They had tried to get me to boost the power in the Cub for a long time. Seeing that new engine setting there sold me. I didn't tell them but I was anxious to try it out.

We also dove into getting Ladonna's Beaver ready for the long trip. Ladonna has been an accomplished pilot for years but has never flown such a distance, nor over such open water or ice. Her and Al will start their honey moon at the cabin, Then fly the Beaver to Banks Island, in the Canadian Arctic. While we coffee break from the maintenance on the Beaver, we pour over her intended route. After leaving the cabin they will stop at Fort Yukon. Then up the Porcupine River to Old Crow in the Yukon Territory. Then over McDougal Pass and on to Aklavaik or Inuvik then Tuktoyaktuk and Cape Parry. The last leg will take them over the Northwest Passage to Sachs Harbour on Banks Island.

As I wiped my hands on an old shop towel, I heard the horn blaring out side. We went to the door to see Ladonna and Al pull up in her Jeep Cherokee. Al opened the back door and out came one of the biggest guys I have ever seen. At least 6'2 or 3 and an easy two hundred thirty or so pounds.

Without waiting for introductions, I met Ian Maguffy. If I thought Al's hand shake firm, I was mistaken. Ian just about put my hand out of commission for good. So this was to be Ladonna's future father in law. We all went into the house and half the people from the day before were still there. Spirit who had preferred to stay with the eats, took one look at Ian and jumped straight onto the middle of his chest. "Where have you been all these months lass?" Right away, I wonder about this remark from Ian. Before I have a chance to say anything

Ladonna called us to supper. The girls had out done themselves. I soon found out why the ancestors had such big meals. It was a celebration. The mood was so festive that I forgot all about Ian and my dog. The food and the spirits lasted well into the night. By morning I was unable to go out to the hanger with the boys.

It was well into the afternoon, before I could get life together enough to go out to the hanger. "How the hell are yeah lad ?" Ian slapped me on the back, nearly bringing up what little breakfast I had eaten. "Fine, Fine." as I tried to get my breath.

I was not too sure about getting along with this guy or not. I should have been a better host but I avoided him for the rest of the day. There remained a lot of work to do on Ladonna's Beaver. The week before I arrived ,the boys painted her. What a beautiful air craft. All bright yellow with black trim on her sides. On each side of the cowl Ladonna had the boys paint the name. "Arctic Spirit". The engine had been gone through by one of the best local aircraft mechanics. Everything that we could think of to do, was done. One of the last things before refueling was to load her up. Ladonna and Al had a lot of supplies and equipment. The wedding gifts were loaded onboard even before the wedding. They could sort that out up at the cabin. We all agreed to give them only the things that they would need, for their winter over on Banks Island.

The Wedding Mass was a grand affair, the little church packed. As the couple went out the door, two Pipers played a tune from the past. I didn't know it at the time but Ian had made the arrangements for the Pipers. I thought it quite fitting.

At the reception, Ian and I raised our glasses in a toast and to my surprise, Ian slipped a necklace around Ladonna's neck. Ladonna gasped and immediately showed it to me. The pendant looked exactly as the coin in the old tin box. It was of gold, and on it, a picture of a king and the numbers 1322.

Before I could really gather it all in, we were all at the hanger as Ladonna fired up the engine. They wasted no time lifting off and were gone.

Chapter 8

Father Paddy

Father Patrick Grif," Paddy" to his friends, was in town and came to the wedding. He knew my father and mother well. An old man now but still spry and ever cheerful. Paddy, Irish/German to the core, had the distinction of being one of the last Sled Dog Priests. For years his only form of winter transportation was by sled. He made his rounds faithfully and even though it was off his circuit, managed a visit with my folks on occasion. Father Paddy and my mother would go on long trips with their teams. Both of them were experts and their teams about the best in the country. On many occasions, I would cheer them on as they raced each other back to the cabin.

He hadn't been to the cabin in years and I could not pass up the opportunity to invite him. I was glad when he accepted straight away. We made arrangements to leave in a day or two as I had to finish business in town.

I also felt compelled to invite Ian to fly up with Joe. I didn't have the heart to tell him that I thought he was too big for the Cub. He really wasn't but I wanted to fly the Cub with the new engine, with out the extra weight.

I hated to leave Spirit behind but Joe would bring her up when he came. Besides Ian and Spirit got along like old friends. With everything settled and Fr Grif loaded in the seat behind me, we took off. The new engine roared as we slipped off the end of the strip. I had never flown the Cub so fast. By the time we reached the cabin strip I was sorry that I hadn't switched engines sooner. I had to adjust my whole way of thinking as I throttled back much sooner than usual.

The kids were gone, in their place a note. As I opened it I had the sinking feeling that I may never see them again. I showed the note to Fr. Paddy and he reassured me that all would be well. We had brought some left overs that the girls packed for us and dined royally on them, then off to bed in the early winter night.

I awoke early to make natures call, only to find the old priest fully in prayer. I tiptoed past him and quietly closed the door. I was not used to having a priest around and tried to stay out of his way, until I got too cold. Once inside, he was still at it, "saying his beads" as my mother would say. I went ahead and built up the fire and was half way through making breakfast, when he spoke. "Ready for Mass?"

I was dumbfounded and dropped the spatula. "Mass?" The old priest continued. "Mass lad, haven't you ever heard of Mass?" Well I had, on Sunday, not the first thing in the morning and certainly not with the likes of me. Breakfast was half done and I could savor the smell of the bacon frying. "Clear the table lad and we'll get on with it, I'm hungry." Not knowing what to say I cleared the table.

Almost before I could set the skillet off the hot spot he had every thing set up using the old table as an alter. My mind and body were not ready for this but how could I refuse such a nice old man? I could smell the bacon as he began, "In the name of the Father and of the Son and of the Holy Spirit." My mind was at once trying to pay attention and at the same time engrossed in the smells of breakfast. Conflicting thoughts raced thru my mind, yes, I wanted to talk with a priest, I thought of the dog, Rachael, Paul, and Simon. I thought of every thing but what I was supposed to. I vaguely recall something about the Gospel. Once again my mind raced to some trivial thing. I saw him raise the Chalice and then every thing seemed to change. There was a flash of light, brighter than I had ever seen. All the world seemed to flash before me. I saw all the family from long ago and I felt as though I were somewhere else. The sky was a bright blue and the stars were out. I was here and there at the same time. Happiness dwelled deep within my being.

The next thing I recall was of Fr Paddy and I calmly eating the much awaited for breakfast. All was silent. I chanced a glance in his direction, he calmly ate as though nothing had happened.

I could hardly contain myself. Words ran around in my head but not out of my mouth. I desperately wanted to talk, to find out what was happening. Fr Paddy broke the ice. "Something you want to say?" I looked at him for a long minute. "What's happening to me father?" "Your eating breakfast lad. Haven't you ever eaten breakfast before?" "No, no, Father, not that." I described the Mass to him ,I told him of the dog and the visits from Rachael, Simon and Paul. I told him of all the stories that my father told me. I even told him of the Spirit Molly, that dad wrote about in his manuscript "Skipping Rock". It must have taken me a long time because when I finished, all he said was "what's for supper ?"

We both cooked, I should say he cooked. All I did was boil up a pot of strong coffee. I thought I was being secretive, as I poured a stiff shot of rum into my cup but he caught me and said "where's mine ?"

We ate in silence. Unable to contain my self any longer I said "well?" "Well what ?" he returned. Father I feel that I am losing touch with reality. "How so lad"?

By this time I started losing patience. "Father I just told you all these stories and you don't think I am losing touch?"

"Well lad, I think it's time for bed." At that the old man slipped out side. As he came in I hoped for some word, any word that would relieve my anxiety's. Not a sound, he slipped into prayer and I went to bed.

We woke early and as I prepared breakfast he finished his prayers. Once again he said Mass. This time there were no lights, no trips off into oblivion, just the same Mass I always remembered.

Dave arrived shortly after breakfast with Spirit and Ian. I was glad to see Spirit but not looking forward to Ian's company. As expected there was the usual slap on the back and crushing handshake. Dave had to catch up with Joe in Fairbanks as soon as possible. After off loading supplies and Ian's bags, he and Father Paddy were gone.

I asked Ian if he had eaten and he said no. I fixed another breakfast as Ian quietly read from some book. Away from other people Ian was a quiet man. He rarely spoke all day. As I rummaged around doing my chores I found a note.

My Dear Paul. I want to take this opportunity to thank you for your gracious company. It is seldom any more that I am able to live as I always liked to. I used to spend time as often as possible with your parents in days gone by. They always treated me well. As for your strange apparitions, they are not strange at all. You are blessed with those who love you and always will. When you strive to be close to God, he will be close to you. It is up to you to pray and try to understand your own life. Thank you once again and may Our Lord keep and bless you always.   Fr Paddy

Chapter 9

Sir Robert the Elder

That evening as Ian continued to read, I slipped on my Parka and Spirit and I went for a walk. At the far end of the strip I looked up to see stars by the thousands in a clear black sky. The Northern Lights danced so close, I felt as though I could reach out and touch them. As I stood there in the silence of the North, Spirit let out a long, drawn out, mournful cry. It surprised me as I had never heard her before. Far off in the distance first one, then another answer followed. We drank in the cold and the night. A satellite passed over head, a glint of light from a far off sun showed its reflection.

Back in the cabin silence was shattered as thunderous snores came from Ian's bed. Spirit curled up behind the stove as I stoked it for the night. One last cup of coffee and I was soon lost in thought. I finally came to the conclusion that God is a wondrous God and that was as much as I could ponder for the night.

The next morning found us up early and at the breakfast table. Spirit had her right paw on Ian's lap. I finally had to ask about the relationship between him and my dog. "I'm glad to oblige" Ian replied as he held out a piece of bacon for Spirit. "Spirit's not your dog! Well not exactly. She's every ones dog lad." I wanted to differ but couldn't. "Ya see lad, she's what we call a Spirit Dog, a protector, a friend and companion. There's lots of dogs but few as special as she is. Have ya ever wondered lad why God gave us dogs? I mean consider this, out of all creatures, dog is closest to man." I had to admit that I had considered the subject. Ian went on,"Dogs are smart, smarter than a lot of us. They have survived for thousands of years and just keep getting closer to us. If it wasn't for dogs a lot of us humans would be very lonely."

I left it to that, for a while at least. I had to do some thinking on that one. Perhaps Ian was right. I thought about Spirit and how she showed up at the cabin and the words of my people about her, on our visit to Point Hope.

Later that morning I left Ian to his book and took Spirit for a brisk cold walk down to the end of the strip. Once again I marveled at the wonders of nature and watched Spirit as she tried to catch a big raven. While lost in thought, I about soiled my long handles as a woman spoke. Turning sharply I recognized Rachael, wrapped in a splendid red blanket. "Good morning Paul, let's walk." Needless to say it took effort for me to reply to her. "Paul why are you so shocked at the site of me?" I stood there dumbfounded. We walked for a few feet before I could get the words out. "Your Rachael!" "Of course I'm Rachael, who did you expect?" Spirit bounded up and knocked her over. They rolled over and over in the new snow, playing like two children. When they were finished she stood, petting Spirit on her big head. All I heard was something like "where have you been? I have been looking for you." They went on and it seemed as though they were conversing in some language that I could not understand.

I pulled my large moose hide mittens off and offered them to her. "I'm not cold Paul, here, feel my hands." She took my hands in hers and the warmth was overpowering. " Paul you are a man of many questions!" I looked at her for what seemed like an eternity and replied, "yes." Then she vanished.

Back in the cabin Ian was still engrossed in his book. I wondered what he was reading. I no sooner had the thought and he piped up " Excellent book." I asked and he commenced to tell me about it. I have been reading the story of our family as your father saw it. There is another side you know." He handed me the book covered in an oil skin wrap. "Keeps it dry." I nodded yes.

I had not opened the cover of our copy of the book after it was published. In fact I had no desire to do so, until this moment. I had spent so much time and effort deciphering my dads scribble. Then all that effort to get it in print.

I opened the cover and the tears welled up inside me. The people, the places, the events. I quickly turned to the story of Jerimiah, Colleen and Broken Eye. I had the feeling while editing dad's manuscript that there was something special about that dog. I quickly handed it back to Ian. I was not ready to tell him of the visit from Rachael and in fact all I wanted was some quiet time. I think that Ian sensed this as we went on about our daily business. He, back to "Skipping Rock" and I to preparing supper.

Once again I could hear the stove chug, this time it was Ian who told the story. "You know lad, I was saying that there is another side to the tale. We both know tales back to John and Ootah but I'll wager that you don't know a one, beyond Sir Robert Laslie Mac Guffok. That's where your side and my side of the family split. You came from Glen Robert the Younger and I came from Sir Robert, his brother." I had to admit that he was right as he went on. " Sir Robert was a rogue from the start. In fact the earliest episode of thievery was when he filched a gold coin from his fathers purse. You know the coin with the picture of a king on it. That's the one that I gave to Ladonna. Sir Robert did not stop at that, he went on, not only to cheat his own brother but swindle every chance he could. If I am not mistaken about the date, the early 1500's were a very good time to flitch the purse of any man not wary enough."

The heat of the coffee and the warmth of the rum put me in the mood to listen. "How about pouring me a stiff portion of that, and skip the coffee." Ian went on. "I hate to admit it but Sir Robert was the scoundrel of the family. He worked his way into the court of the English King and by what ever means he could, he was Knighted. Can you imagine that? A sell out of a good Scottish family to the English. Any way lad, needless to say in the end he not only lost his fortune but his life as well. He was eventually hanged by the same people that had purchased his soul."

Ian went on till the wee hours of the morning. He said that Sir Robert had three sons and five daughters. He had married well, perhaps helping him to achieve his status. His middle son known as Mac took the brunt of his fathers downfall.

Chapter 10

Bad News

We both could hardly hold our heads up the next morning. One of the boys was due to fly in and pick Ian up. The pre dawn broke with fog coming off the river so thick we couldn't see half of the strip. At that time of the year its not uncommon for the ice to break in places and let the moisture out in the form of fog. The temperature was standing at about minus 26. Other wise you could see the stars in places through the breaks in the fog cover.

Ian quietly sang some ancient Scottish tune as he packed his bag. I hated to see him go. We were just getting acquainted. We ate breakfast in silence knowing that we must meet again and carry on the tales. Spirit laid her head in his lap as he gently stroked her ears. You could almost touch the dogs sadness.

We were glad that the fog had lifted as one of the boys approached off the end of the strip. All too soon Joe landed and with out shutting down the engine, reached out and handed me a letter. I off loaded supplies as Ian climbed aboard and in a blink they were gone, leaving great swirls of fog behind them.

Spirit and I were alone. The cabin was eerily quiet as I looked at the postage mark on the letter. Some place in Canada that I was not familiar with. No return address. Curiosity getting the better of me I tore it open.

Dear Dad, Just a short note to let you know that we are well and happy. Al is off to some remote location on Banks Island, while I sit here trying to decide my next move. Usually I am with Al and of course that is preferred to sitting here. The news is that you are going to be a grand pa. I thought I was pregnant but waited a while until we could get to the little clinic here in Sachs Harbour.

I much prefer counting Musk Ox, to life in this little out post on the edge of the Arctic ice, but oh well. Love and kisses Ladonna

The boys still didn't have any children and this was the greatest surprise. I never dreamed that Ladonna would be the first. I couldn't contain my self and started talking to Spirit out loud. "What do you think of that? Ladonna's going to have a baby!" Spirit just looked at me with that sideways glance of hers. like what are you talking about?

Thoughts of my wife and what she would say about it flashed across my mind. Marie would love the idea of grand children. I started thinking about going to Banks Island until I went out side and the bitter cold hit me. The distance was too far for this old guy in that little Cub. But then again I have flown in worse conditions. I put it out of my head and stoked the old stove for supper.

April found me basking in temperatures in the thirties and forties during the day. Though I am seldom bored I looked forward to another visit from Ian. He had sent a letter from somewhere around Baffin Island saying that he had a chance to make it out for a month. The last time that I had heard from Ladonna, she said that she was planning on a return to Fairbanks. Ladonna said that she did not want to have the baby on the island ,though she had the best regards for her medic.

I thought that she would fly out on one of the local commercial operations and leave her Beaver on Banks Island. I knew that I hadn't raised a fool for a pilot, so put these thoughts from my mind and readied the cabin for visitors.

The night of the fourth, Spirit disappeared. I have been looking for her for a week now with no luck. I readied the Cub and flew a search pattern that went far beyond where I would expect her to be. Disappointment at her absence left me very lonely.

On the seventh day after Spirit disappeared I had a visit from an old friend from Wiseman. I could her him coming a mile off. I looked out the window to see him flying up from the South, snow machine wide open. Jumping off before he came to a complete stop and out of breath, he hollered at me like I was deaf. "Paul I got a message on the radio that they want you in Fairbanks A.S.A.P." I got him calmed down enough to come into the cabin. "They think Ladonna's down." I had never seen him so excited. I quickly poured a stiff shot in his hot cup and asked again what he was going on about. "I don't know, the message was garbled with static and all I got was for you to get on down there. Some thing about Ladonna down."

Sam helped me get my arctic gear together and ready the Cub. He said he would close up the cabin and keep an eye out for Spirit as he helped me break the ski's loose from the ice crust. I made a mental check of all my gear as the engine warmed up. With a wave, I gunned the old girl and lifted off at least 30 feet sooner than usual.

The flight to Fairbanks was over before I realized it. I took one round of my home strip and dropped her in. The boys had the hanger door open and I taxied straight in.

The boys took me to the house, and once thru the door a whole bunch of people quietly greeted me. Old friends of Marie and I as well as Fr. Paddy and almost all of the friends of the kids. They got me seated and proceeded to tell me that indeed Ladonna was missing. Apparently she had decided that the weather report was good enough. With Al's reluctant blessing she took off, intending to follow the original flight route. Al was on the search from the Canadian end and the boys as well as the Civil Air Patrol had already flown the route more than once. She had been missing for seven days. I asked them, a little irked, "why in the sam hell, didn't you notify me?"

They gave the lame excuse that they didn't want to worry me. "Worry hell, I need to be out there looking." I suppose I was a little distraught as Ladonna's friends tried to calm me. Joe told me that they were loaded and ready to leave as soon as I was. They wanted to wait till dawn to go but I said that I would take the Cub and go now. "Well dad, let us boys get you refueled and we will go. Not much chance of seeing anything till day light". I thought that was kind of stupid and wondered if they ever thought that she might have a fire and be seen.

Chapter 11

Looking for Ladonna

We left at about 10 Pm. Ladonna's girl friends packed each of us a whole bag full of sandwiches and several thermos's of coffee. Once in the air we fanned out in a formation that would allow us to see more area. We flew up to Fort Yukon and refueled. In the air again, we headed up the Porcupine River intending to go as far as the border. The few times in my life that I have flown this, has always left me thinking of it as being the most pristine place on earth. The boys were very familiar with this area as they did a lot of flying of their clients in this direction. The night sky was as crystal clear as I have ever seen it. The star light bounced off of the snow lighting the area as though there were a full moon. If there was any one down there, we should be able to spot them. Once I caught a glimpse of fire light and banked for a closer look but it disappeared.

I couldn't help but think that it was the beginning of the 8th day. I hoped that she had all her survival gear and further, I couldn't stand the thought of her and the baby down there alone and injured.

We returned to Fort Yukon and refueled. We have many friends in the town, so getting a good breakfast was no problem. We got hold of the authorities on the Canadian side and they had called off the search. Al and some of his friends were going up to McDougall Pass on their next leg. The boys and I decided that we would go across the border and search between Old Crow and the pass. Fortified with fresh coffee and the remainder of the food the girls packed, we took off. We widened our search pattern and dropped into Old Crow to refuel. We searched right up to the pass and by chance met two other aircraft coming from the other direction. All of us fanned out even further. The weather was crystal clear and I saw one of the craft bank to the right just out side of Old Crow, Most of the mountains around the area are 4000 to 5000 feet or so in elevation. As he headed toward one of the peaks I could see a flash of light off of a wing down below.

Ladonna, I thought, It's got to be Ladonna. We all landed at Old Crow which is just a few miles from the downed plane. The people were kind enough to lend us their snow machines and four of us with one of the local natives sped to the site.

The plane was hard to spot from the ground, so we sent one of the machines back to get his plane in the air and act as spotter. In about two hours he was flying in circles about half a mile from us. That was all we needed. We had to leave the machines and trek through knee high snow the last 500 or so feet. We were lucky to find the plane at all in this great expanse of wilderness. One partially snow covered wing stuck out of a rocky area. The Beaver was on its belly and healed over about 40 degrees. One wing was broken off and the nose caved in around the engine. We pried the door open to find one very cold and unconscious woman. We had quite a time getting her out of the plane but managed with the help of three more natives that came up, following our tracks. They brought a long sled and strapped to it, we managed to get her into Old Crow. Once there she started to respond to our voices. We tried to get some hot liquid into her but could not. We loaded her into Joe's Otter and headed for Fort Yukon. The Physician Assistant stationed at Fort Yukon got an IV going and started treatment to warm her up. He checked the babies heart rate and suggested that we fly her back to Fairbanks.

It was two days before she really started to come out of it. As Al and I sat with her she kept mumbling something about Spirit. On the third day she was fully awake. She lost a couple of toes to frost bite and a few pounds of weight as well as multiple cuts and bruises but other than that, her and the baby were fine.

Her friends and family crowded into the living room of our house, all wanting to hear what happened. As she laid back in my big recliner, Al mothered her to no end. Ladonna said that she had an uneventful trip and had planned to drop into Old Crow, for the night. She could see a cloud bank ahead and tried to circle it but the Beaver started to ice up. Before she knew it, she had lost control and bellied into the side of a mountain.

Ladonna went on to say that she could not get out of the Beaver. She told us that the cold was unmerciful. She did have some room to move about in the Beaver but could not reach the radio to make a distress call. The food that she brought with her was enough for a couple of days but she could not find the survival kit with more food. The emergency stove was useless because she was afraid it would ignite the dripping aircraft fuel. Ladonna said that thoughts of her baby as well as Al kept passing before her. Then just when distress started to over take her, Spirit came and kept her warm. She said that Rachael also talked to her, telling stories to keep her awake. She even said that Rachael sang to her. Ladonna lost track of time as one day went into another. Spirit stayed with her and she kept hope that we would find her.

There were a few shaking heads among her friends and doubtful glances from others but the family believed. Every one looked at me as I said "Why else would that darn dog leave me?" I left it at that, as Ian winked. Fr Paddy just smiled.

In the days that followed, guilt and depression overcame Ladonna. She wished that she would have listened to Al, when he had argued so hard for her not to fly the Beaver. She was also depressed at the thought of losing her plane. I attempted to console her in different ways, even telling her that another aircraft could have gone down as well. What ever I said left her in the same frame of mind. Ian and Al had to get back to their work and most of us just wanted for things to return to normal. Even though I wanted to stay with Ladonna I felt compelled to return to the cabin.

I waited for several more days, then with a sudden bolt of inspiration asked Ladonna to come along. At first she appeared to be strongly opposed. By that time she was about 7 months along with her baby and objected to going back into the bush, at that late date. Not only that but she came up with as many excuses as she could.

Being the fool that I am, I managed to over power her reluctance and she finally agreed. Still with 2 or 3 months left, her doctor gave her a clean bill of health to go. The boys and I laid supplies into the Cub and after lunch they brought her into the hanger. I sat in the back seat. When she saw that, she pitched a fit. "I am not going to fly! How could you even think of that"? We let her go on for a few minutes. When she finally stopped her objections, we calmly explained that it was in her best interest to take the controls now. Ladonna finally and reluctantly agreed. I could see how tense she was as she got in. While the engine warmed up, her shoulders appeared to relax a bit. Ladonna poured the power to the Cub and we took straight into the air.

We passed over the Yukon River and she hollered back "thanks dad." We continued on in the cloudless midday sky. I am proud of her, Ladonna can be stubborn at times but will rise to challenges when she needs to.

It was no surprise as I looked out the left side window and saw Spirit below. What was a surprise, was the dog with her.

Ladonna dropped onto the strip as gracefully as ever. At the cabin end of the strip, she swung the Cub around and killed the engine. We got out to the greetings of two magnificent animals. Ladonna wrapped her arms around Spirit as the other dog sat quietly in the background. I gave my thanks and I ruffed Spirit's big head. The two dogs walked ahead of us to the cabin, Spirit and the other dog, shoulder to shoulder. "Looks like they are old friends," Ladonna said. I opened the door and both dogs calmly walked in as though they owned the place. I stoked the fire to take the cold out of the place, they just sat. Out of the corner of my eye I could see Ladonna with her face in Spirit's long fur.

Ladonna did the cooking after I saw her scrape the old skillet, of the remains of last months meals. The two dogs laid behind the chugging stove, each with one paw over the others. As I watched them I felt that Spirits friend, looked strangely familiar. It was obvious that he was a big male. His eyes were that of a wolf and the one on the left wandered but otherwise he appeared to be a highland sheep dog. A great scar covered the left side of his head from above the eye to his cheek.

We sat with our coffee after supper and watched as the two dogs stretched from time to time but never seemed to part. After one particularly long stretch, the big male extended his neck and laid his head over the chest of the sleeping Spirit.

"Dad, I think I know who he is. He's Colleen's dog, Broken Eye." Instantly, out of nothing, Rachael appeared at the table. A beautiful woman, with long black hair, olive skin, dressed in quill decorated buckskins and wrapped in a red blanket.

The dogs rose to greet her as she spoke. "You are correct Ladonna. This is indeed Broken Eye. These two have been mates for many years.

Usually where you see one, you will see the other. Broken Eye has been on one of his assignments. That is the reason you haven't seen him before."

Not wanting to forget my manners, I offered Rachael a cup of my finest pot boiled bush coffee. She waved her hand in refusal but asked if we had any tea. "Your mother used to make me tea when I visited her, besides I never developed a taste for coffee." Rachael retold the story of Broken Eye's adventures with Jerimiah and Colleen. It was the same story that my dad told in his manuscript. Rachael kept us enthralled with a few more tales of Broken Eye, ones that we didn't know. Before we had a chance to talk more and fulfill the many questions we had, she petted Spirit and Broken Eye, gave them a big hug and vanished.

Chapter 12

Broken Eye's Return

We took many short walks over the next days. They were not far as Ladonna tired easily. The dogs ranged far and wide searching out any and all little critters. It is always fun to watch dogs chasing something, that they have little hope in catching. It appeared to be a cat and mouse game. Once Spirit spotted some tasty morsel she stood high on her hind legs and came down hard on her front paws. I just know this scares the daylights out of the little critters. Spirit hopes that it will frighten the critter so much that it wont move. Most of the time it does and then Broken Eye joins the chase. They scurried around for four or five minutes going this way and that before giving up. It's never long and the chase is on again in some other location.

Time passed quickly and our time alone together drew to a close. I relished all the things we did together, especially the long evenings setting at the table, with both of us writing by the old kerosene lamp. Once in a while Ladonna would bend over my shoulder, reading what I wrote. She occasionally would offer suggestions to better turn a phrase. At first I rebelled , but soon realized that it would be easier to finally put into print, if it was done correctly the first time. I recalled how much difficulty I had deciphering dad's writings.

Early one morning Joe slipped his Otter onto the strip. We went out to meet him and Ladonna beamed from ear to ear as she caught a glimpse of Al in the cockpit next to Joe. Joe and I off loaded the supplies as Ladonna and Al went into the cabin.

Supper that night was a joyous occasion. Al did the cooking and did it well indeed. I for one had no idea that he knew any thing about it. He had fresh beef flown in from the lower forty eight, as well as fresh greens. These things are available in Fairbanks but it was the idea that he would go to such trouble. To top it off he unpacked real ice cream from it's resting place in dry ice. I felt stuffed and couldn't thank Al for the meal enough.

Day light in May is an ever increasing affair. Joe threw some supplies in our packs after supper and to give Ladonna and Al some privacy, we took off on a fishing trip. Joe and I took the Cub, as I would need its short landing ability, to glide into a short scree filled landing spot. Dad had taken me there many times in my youth. It is little known, in fact I really doubt that any one knows of it. As we flew deeper into the Brooks Range I marveled at the Dall sheep high on the rocky slopes. I made a few passes in and out of a tight pass and before us lay the nameless lake. We landed with inches to spare, tied down the Cub and slept under a wing for the night.

I awoke to the aroma of strong coffee, as Joe had been up for several hours. The crackle of trout frying in the camp skillet brought me fully awake. Morning ablutions done, I approached the small fire. Joe knew well the fine art of camp cooking, got it from me, I suspect. He slowly turned the fillets and handed me a cup at the same time. I tipped the pot and the aroma spilled out in a cascade of black gold. Breakfast of fried trout and potatoes left me ready to fish.

The small mountain lake is about fifty feet wide, two hundred feet long and we guess thirty or so feet deep. There are several ledges of rock jutting into it around the shore. It drops off to it's depth fairly fast. The water is clear as crystal all the way to the bottom. A very small stream feeds it at the upper end and the lower end outlets much the same. I have seen it a time or two in the winter and have never seen it frozen over. I assume that an underground hot spring also feeds it. We took trout as big as twelve pounds out of the small lake but many six or eight pounders can be seen as well. They are weary, you have to fish this lake with finesse. They rise to clip low flying mosquitos and I tie on one of my small flies. A few whips of the rod and my fly is picked out of the air by a high jumper.

There is no darkness to speak of but the nights are cold and beautiful, as only the brightest of stars can be seen. We laughed and joked and ate our fill of fish. Taking advantage of the fire, we dried a great amount to take with us. After three days we tired of fishing and decided to go home. We were in high spirits as we packed up our catch and gear. I laughed at some joke that Joe told as I warmed the engine. The short strip had a slight downward slope to it as I took off at full throttle. At about fifty feet of altitude the engine quit dead.

It was too late to do any thing but drop out of the sky. We hit hard on large boulders and flipped. The last thing I recall was hitting the instrument panel.

When I awoke I was on the ground with oil dripping on my face. I reached up to wipe it off and came away with blood and oil mixed together in a reddish black goo. Joe was nowhere in sight. I called out to him and had only silence for an answer. My left arm was twisted in several places and as I attempted to stand, pain shot up my right leg and I fell. When I once again woke, I called out to Joe again. Still no answer. As I laid there, I looked around in disbelief. The Cub was up side down. Both wings were folded in at an odd angle. I could just see around the engine that was over me supported by the bent prop. The fuselage was bent over a bolder. I slipped from under the engine with only inches to spare. Crawling away from my bird I gained a safer spot.

Time slipped until I became colder. I tried to reach into the Cub and get out my sleeping bag with no luck. I recall slipping into some twilight of sleep where I thought my folks were talking to me. It wasn't them. I woke with a start to see Joe standing over me. He was fine except for a big lump on his head and a few cuts.

Joe said that he must have been out cold for a while. He had called to me but had no answer. He said that he eventually managed to get his bearings and was glad to have found me alive. We were in trouble to say the least. As I said before I doubted that any one would look for us at the lake.

While all this was going on, another story unfolded. Ladonna went into labor. They waited for us to return for as long as they could, and Al had some major decisions at hand. Al had been with Ladonna many times as she flew the Beaver but had never flown himself. He thought many times about learning but always found some reason to put it off. Ladonna at first, thought it to be perhaps a false labor as she was not yet due. Then she thought it might be food poisoning from eating food cooked in my skillet. Al was beside himself. How stupid could he be to have his wife in two perilous situations, in such a short period of time. While he kicked himself over and over again, Ladonna worried about us. Finally she asked Al to get her to the radio in the Beaver.

On our end, Joe scrapped material from my Cub for splints. He had me trussed up like a Thanksgiving Turkey. Despite the big lump on his head he was fine. Joe made our camp as comfortable as he could. We were lucky that none of our gear or dried fish, had been lost. Joe was able to fish and had continued luck in bringing in some big ones. Fire wood was the problem. At that altitude above the tree line, he found very little left to burn. He could use small pieces of the Cub but I hesitated to allow that. We had a few discussions over that. I kept insisting that I owned that plane all my life and she would fly again. He refused to believe that at all. I said that when we got out of our situation, I would have a helicopter come up and bring her back to Fairbanks. Joe thought I was nuts. "You have had that piece of junk for so many years, I think that you have that thing attached to your butt. It's just junk dad, well get you another one." I came back with "I don't want another one, I will fly that one again." While that was going on, Joe decided that he would have to go farther afield for wood.

Here and there and few and far between, one could find small pieces of wood. There certainly were no trees within ten or so miles. Finding enough wood for our need's would be a major project. I was of no help, but our camp was close enough for me to fish if I took my time and didn't spook them with too much casting.

Ladonna said that her pains were so close together and so intense, that she had Al carry her to her plane. She stood outside instructing Al on the operation of the radio. No one answered their call. Al took Ladonna back to the cabin and continued to try and raise some one. Finally he raised an aircraft far off to the South. He later told me that he thought it to be a commercial air liner. His message was relayed to Fairbanks. Dave flew in with one of Ladonna's friends, a nurse, and Ladonna as well as Al, were taken to the hospital in Fairbanks. I was eventually to have a surprise.

The Civil Air Patrol wasted no time in launching a search for us. Unfortunately they had no idea as to which area to search. In our haste to leave Ladonna and Al on their own, we neglected to tell them where we were going.

Joe took some of the dried fish, water and little else with him. His plan was to go down the mountain far enough to find a supply of wood to bring back. This should have taken no more than one long day. On day three, I knew that we were in for it. I had all the dried fish to eat plus water from the lake. All the food that we brought with us was gone. I found my self back in the need for prayer. It's funny that most of us wait until we are in deep trouble, before we turn to the source of all goodness and blessing. From the time that I had the encounter, that I had when Fr Paddy visited me, I had prayed on occasion. That was an exercise in guilt for all the times that I had failed to give proper due. This was different. On day five, I started to give up hope. On day ten, I was very tired of fish. On day fifteen, I started to think of getting out of there. I knew that it was at least seventy five miles to the nearest help. I was able to walk slowly with a limp and pain but my arm was definitely going to need some real attention. I was sure that something had happened to Joe. One minute I thought about walking out of there and the next, about staying with the plane. I finally packed my compass, the last of the matches, the remaining dried fish, the old coffee pot and my sleeping bag in a small roll and said goodby to my old friend. Down the mountain a ways, I looked back at her twisted back and vowed to come back and get her.

It was going to be tougher than I thought. Age was catching up with me. The pain in my leg increased with each step. When I reached the bottom of the canyon I could see a line of stunted willows. With a painful slowing gate, I reached them in several hours. I was pooped as I slung my bag to the ground and laid my head on it. I awoke some time later to find Broken Eye standing over me. He had a look on his face like, what kept you? I buried my head in his fur and wept in thanks giving for some one to talk to. "Well boy what are we going to do now?" He cocked his head to the side as if pointing the way. "That's not the way" I told him. He started to walk in the direction he wanted. I picked my things up and started in the direction that I wanted. Broken Eye came toward me like he was going to attack. Instead he latched onto my good arm, pulling me in his direction. I stopped for a minute trying to think things through. I said one prayer and followed. Sure that we were going in the wrong direction, I collapsed in fatigue. The going had been rough. The muskeg, small streams, and occasional rocks took their toll on my body. "That's it, not another step." I sat down and looked at my boots. I had needed a new pair long before this trip but as usual waited to buy something until forced to. Kind of like, one of these days I'm going to become a procrastinator. I guess Broken Eye took pity on me as he came back and laid down with me. I was sick of fish, but forced some down any way. I gave a big hunk to Broken Eye and he seemed to relish it. In fact he begged for more. We slept for a while but soon the big dog shook me as if to say get up. For two more days I half walked and was literally dragged. I had lost all track of time. I think it must have been somewhere around sixteen or seventeen days since the crash.

The CAP and the Air Force had flown search missions in all directions without any sign of us. When they gave up, Dave, with Al as spotter, continued to fly patterns in ever increasing circles.

Broken Eye and I walked for two more days. About the time that the fish ran out Broken Eye started hunting. I rested in the shade of a stunted conifer for a while. Broken Eye disappeared. He returned in a short while with a Ptarmigan. It wasn't long and he returned with another, then another. By the time he finished we had enough for a meal for the both of us. I broke branches from the puny trees, built a fire and roasted the birds to fine order. We feasted on the first real meat in a long while. I didn't care if I ever saw another fish.

The morning of the twentieth day, found us crossing another stream. When I reached the half way point I looked up to see Spirit on the shore waiting. My spirits soared as I knew that God had something up his sleeve for me. It was a joyous greeting that she gave us. The two pranced around like they were on a picnic.

Little did I know that Joe had been found the day before not too far from my location. He later told me that he had not lost his way entirely, but did get turned around. Joe's head injury was worse than we had thought. He had lost his memory for a long time and was surprised not only to see Spirit but that his beard had grown considerably. Evidently Spirit had done for him, what Broken Eye had done for me.

The dogs and I sat on a long flat sand bar. I must have been a sight. My boots as well as clothes were in shreds, my beard long. The sky appeared a bright blue in the morning Sun as the first aircraft I had seen, buzzed over head. At first I stood in disbelief as the plane went out of sight. Then as quickly as it left it swung around to the South

49

and came back. It was no more than twenty feet over my head as it about blew me over. One more pass and it glided onto the bar. One of the Bush Pilots helped me inside as I looked around for the dogs. They were gone.

Chapter 13

New Life

It took weeks but Joe and I finally managed to recover. Joe's head injury required extensive surgery. Apparently he had developed a lot of pressure in his skull and in the end, doctors felt that he was lucky to be alive. There were many weeks before his memory fully returned. I had to have multiple surgeries to fix my fractured arm and will have limited use of it in the future.

We both went back home and were taken care of by friends and professional help that we hired. Over time, I grew especially fond of Dakota, the nurse that cared for me. Dakota is a few years younger than I am but that doesn't seem to bother her. She expresses a love for flying, the life I choose to live and has been a big help to me. She is a beautiful woman.

The real loves of my life are the twins. Megan and Elizabeth. I am sorry that I was not here when they were born but I get to spend time with them now. They were born shortly after our crash and are now about six months old. Ladonna is here with the girls, while Al finishes his work on Banks Island. I am glad that we built such a big house, as it is large enough for all of us. Ian took time from his job and stayed quite a while. I felt regretful when he left. He is as proud of the twins as I am.

I spent long hours in our hanger working on the Cub. What a mangled mess. I was bound and determined to get her back in the air. I had healed to the point of not needing a nurse but prolonged letting Dakota go. She still mothered me at times but more and more just spent time with me. Dakota had a lot of questions about flying, sometimes more than I wanted to answer. I recalled the early days as I learned to fly, by just such questions.

Ladonna brought the twins to see the planes often. Even at their early age they seemed to like touching the stretched fabric. Dakota took one girl and I the other. Dakota seemed to have a large command of aviation language, as she showed the girls each part.

The boys were politely overpowered in their objections by Dakota. They absolutely thought I was wasting my time on the Cub. Dakota hired one of the local helicopter recovery teams to bring the wreckage back. I drew a map of the area and amazingly they found the Cub straight away. After a few calls, we found another Cub to use for parts. One of my old friends had her stuck in the back corner of his hanger. It hadn't flown for years. Mine would never be the same again but we used a lot of her in the new plane. We were able to salvage the new engine that the boys gave me, as except for the prop, it wasn't damaged. This new Cub has STOL wings. This allows for even shorter strip landings. We also updated the communications equipment, as well as a rescue beacon.

One day Ladonna showed me a stack of uncashed pay checks. All of them belonging to Dakota. When I asked her about them she had no answer. When I asked her where Dakota had been going, she still couldn't tell me. I started wondering if Dakota was another spirit in my life. Secretly, I hoped that she was not. I could not imagine Dakota not being around. Much to my relief Dakota came thru the door. When I asked her about the checks she just shrugged her shoulders and gave me that coy smile of hers. I just left it at that and asked her out to dinner.

Dakota Jean Fitzpatrick and I were married in the little Catholic Church on Cushman street. The wedding was private and we were lucky enough to have Fr Paddy to do the honors.

I had longed to return to the cabin, ever since I left on our fateful flight. I assumed that Dakota would want to go to some exotic island for our honey moon but assumptions are often wrong. She couldn't wait to see the cabin. By this time a new spring had arrived and all the gardens of Fairbanks were well out of the ground.

One more surprise awaited me. One bright sunny late spring day, the kids, with smiles on their faces, took me out to the porch. I grumbled a bit and looked around, wondering what they were up to. They told me to be patient. I waited but nothing happened. About the time I started back into the house, they told me to look. Off in the distance, a small plane appeared in the bright sky. As it came closer, I could not believe my eyes.

My Cub dropped onto the strip with the ease of a Gull. As the pilot taxied up to us and cut the engine, out popped Dakota. I just stood there with my mouth hanging open. "Where in the hell did you learn to fly"? Was about all I could get out. She bound up to me and threw her arms around me saying, "Like it?" I was still wondering where the hell she learned to fly, or how, or when. We walked around the Cub with arms around each other. The kids were cracking up with laughter. It appeared that I was the only one that was in the dark of recent events.

The Cub was beautiful. I had never seen her in such a fresh light. I knew she was about finished as we had her together with a fresh coat of paint, in our own hanger. Dave had taken her out on her trials and said that he left her at the airport to have something checked. Little did I know that Dakota had soloed in her. All the time that she said she was going here or there she had instead, taken lessons.

Now I knew that it was time to return to the cabin. The boys and I packed Dakota's things in the Cub and Ladonna planned on following in Joe's Otter. Dave planned on staying behind taking care of the business. However Ladonna took off before us, with Joe holding the twins in the rear of the aircraft.

I reluctantly took the back seat as Dakota went through her pre flight check. Once ready, I was to be her first passenger. I felt much as my dad must have felt, flying with me for the first time. My advantage was in the fact that Dakota had her license.

The rebuilt Cub lifted off as sweetly as ever. The engine applying full force to the lift. Once at altitude, Dakota trimmed her back for a comfortable ride. I relaxed as I realized I had a flying partner. The ground below revealed stunted trees as we went over the Chena River. Dakota circled the town one time giving us a good view of the Alaska Range with Mt Denali's glacier encrusted peak at 20,320 feet. The day was clear in a bright blue sky as we went out over the serpentine Tannana River, before circling back for our trip to the cabin.

The new STOL wings were much like a Gull's as Dakota slid the Cub onto the strip and swung in next to Ladonna's bird. Once she cut the engine, I got out and as a joke kissed the earth under my feet.

I still wonder if Dakota appreciated that. She and Ladonna walked off, arm in arm after giving me a dirty look. All things considered I really would fly with her any time.

Things were much as I had left them. Dave had flown up with out our knowledge some time before and restocked the place. Once inside, Ladonna told me that he had restocked the wood pile, as some one had used the cabin the previous winter. It has been a long established custom in the North to restock a cabin if one who needed it can. I hope that who ever needed the place was comfortable.

I had the privilege of stoking up the fire in the old stove. Dakota busied herself unpacking. Ladonna seemed to enjoy telling Dakota that she needed to watch my sanitation of the skillet. The twins busied themselves crawling on the bare floor. Joe catered to their every need. I told him that he would make a good wife. That's all Ladonna needed to jibe him on his bachelorhood.

A fantastic supper was prepared by Dakota and I marveled at her finesse in the kitchen. She had brought a big honey smoked ham with all the fixings and fix it well she did. About all she would allow me to do, was stoke the stove. Between this and watching the grand kids I admired this woman, who had become such a major part of my life.

Warmed by the stove on the cool spring night and a wee shot of rum in our cups, we listened as Dakota told her story.

She began slowly, telling us that she was born on a reservation in South Dakota. "My grand father on my mothers side, was Three Feathers son of White Horse. Mother and father worked hard supporting my five brothers and sisters during the depression. Dad always said that he felt blessed by all that he had. He was a devout Catholic but lived too far from town to be a part of a church community. Mother taught us our ABC's and gave us the best of her faith. My great grand dad on my fathers side, served in the Union Army during the Civil War, losing a leg at some battle. No one ever said which battle". I got up and poured us another cup of coffee from the stove. I sat down close to her, she went on. "My fathers family came to Virginia in the late 1700's and fought in the Revolutionary War. Before that the family came from Ireland".

As she went on, we found out how she became a nurse. 'My first husband was in the Air Force and worked at Torbay Newfoundland.

We stayed there for about six years. That was long enough for me to get my nursing degree in St Johns. Jack was killed in Vietnam. After that I found myself at loose ends and decided to come North".

Chapter 14

Return to Point Hope

The kids stayed for a few days more and we regretted seeing them go. Dakota and I had the cabin and our lives once again to our selves.

Lazy days melted into weeks of a beautiful arctic summer. The kids came up with resupply's and additional fuel on occasion. Dakota used up fuel as fast as we could resupply it. Many mornings I would wake to the sound of the Cub engine winding up. Each flight that she took found her further afield. I spent the time alone writing as she unfolded her adventures before me. By mid summer she had enough of local flying and wanted to stretch out further. I had wanted to return to Point Hope ever since I left and suggested that we make the trip.

The trip was uneventful as we took the same route as I had made before. This time we avoided the bad fuel. We stopped more often and spent nights in the small tent, listening to squadrons of mosquitos bombarding an otherwise quiet night. Dakota snuggled closer while calls of the wild wolves occasionally pierced our senses. This I rather liked but always thought of Broken Eye and Spirit and wished that I could see them again. Dakota remained skeptical of our family tales of these two dogs but said she had an open mind.

Point Hope loomed ahead as Dakota flew a straight course along the shore of the Chukchi Sea from Kivalina. The sea put up small white caps while Dakota adjusted her path in the cross wind. Though I had flown all my life, I enjoyed being in the rear seat for a change. Occasionally I bent over the front seat, giving advise in her ear. Most of the time I just sat back and enjoyed the ride.

She came into Point Hope on a cross wind, touching the left wheel then the right. Perfect as far as I was concerned. I had to remark that I could have done it better, with a wink of course. We tied the Cub down and started to unload our stuff as a small crowd of cousins came up to us in joyful spirits.

That evening the sun dipped low but never disappeared. We sat around a driftwood fire, eating and telling stories, until we could not keep our eyes open. This time I brought the largest supply of dried arctic char and moose that I could stuff into the Cub. There were also other small gifts that the children especially liked. The female cousins liked the gold nugget charms and the men laid into the ammunition of varying calibers, that I knew they would like.

The only thing missing was my great aunt. Her son told of her death. He said that she was a wise woman and all of the people mourned their loss. I felt the loss also, I had great respect for her. The passing of this old person was one more loss of ancient ways.

The second evening was much the same as the first. My great aunt's son, Ben Bear Hunter, now one of the elder story tellers asked me about the great dog. Dakota held one of the young ones as I told of the crash and rescue. I told them of Spirit and Broken Eye and how they saved us. The old man nodded his head in agreement and said that he has also seen Broken Eye. In fact he said that he has seen that dog more than he has seen Spirit. Dakota thought perhaps that he was stretching the yarn a bit.

Ben or Ben Hunter as he is now known went on. "The last time I saw the great dog that you say is Broken Eye, was on a hunt. Four of us were on an ice flow far out to the West, almost to Siberia. Our outboard motor had quit, while we hunted the Great White Bear." I thought this might be a long tale so braced myself as he went on. " We pulled the boat up onto an ice flow, to see if we could fix it. One of the men fired up the gas stove to make coffee and while he pumped it up, it exploded." At this, all the people leaned forward and listened intently, as if they had not heard the story before. Ben went on. "The explosion blew the man backward, setting his parka on fire. Before we could help him, we saw the Great White Bear off in the distance coming toward us." Ben got to his feet and acted out the event, as one of the cousins began to beat a small drum in unison. "Two of the men tried to beat out the fire, as I raised my riffle. The Great White Bear came closer. The more the burning man screamed in pain, the faster the bear ran. Just as the bear came into range, the big dog Broken

57

Eye, as you called him appeared out of nowhere. The Great White Bear stopped as the dog charged him. He raised up onto his hind legs." Ben raised his old arms as high as they would go and went on. "The big dog charged the bear taking out part of the Great White Bear's belly. The bleeding bear dropped and quickly turned on the big dog." At that, Ben Bear Hunter stopped talking, the drummer quit drumming and both sat down in silence.

Ben's oldest daughter brought him a fresh cup of coffee, while we sat waiting in rapt attention for the rest of the story. Ben sat in silence looking off to the open sea. Dakota looked at me with her puzzled look. I slowly raised my hand, slightly, wait. I did not want to break the spell. Ben Bear Hunter was a master story teller if I have ever heard one.

Even though it was summer, a cold breeze floated in from the sea as Ben got up. He began to dance, slowly, as the drummer beat a rhythm. The dance went as only the Inuit people can dance. Short, jerking motions in time with the drum. As quickly as he started, he stopped dancing and once again told the story. "The bear slashed at the dog with his great claws and foamed at the mouth. He tried to get the dog with his teeth. The dog lunged time and time again at the bear. The bear roared and raged as the dog kept going for its throat. The bear came down on the dog with a mighty blow that sent the dog reeling. The dog came back time and time again. The bear tired, as each swipe of the claws and snap of the jaws missed the dog. With one final lunge the dog grabbed the throat of the Great White Bear and did not let go. The bear swung his head back and forth trying to shake the dog loose. It finally collapsed to the ice in silence." Once again the old man sat down looking off into the distance reliving every memory of the event.

With the driftwood fire rekindled, the story went on. I watched Dakota as she hung on every word. "The burned man lay unconscious as we started for the bear. The great dog disappeared as quickly as he appeared. Once skinned out, the Great White Bear measured two men wide and more than two men long, blood covered the ice in every direction." Being a nurse, Dakota couldn't contain her self any longer. "What about the poor man?" The people gasped and every one looked at her, as though she had committed a great sin, interrupting a story teller. The old man just smiled at her. "We fixed the motor, put the bear meat and skin in the boat, left the exploded stove on the ice, put the man in the boat and came home."

The story teller got up and went home, so did the rest of us. As we were about to go to sleep, Dakota asked me if all that was really true. I turned over and fell fast asleep, dreaming of the Great White Bear.

I dreaded leaving but did not want to wear out the welcome. We readied the Cub and the family came to give us a send off. As usual there were gifts. This time it was Dakota that received most of them. We had to find a spot in the cramped Cub for a new parka and mukluks, Dakota could not get over the beauty of these precious gifts. There remained one more surprise. Ben Bear Hunter and another man came carrying a large bundle. They dropped it to the ground and opened it. Dakota now owned the largest white bear skin that I have ever seen. Several men and I rolled it into the smallest package possible and secured it under the Cub. Before Dakota climbed in to the cockpit, her and the old man embraced. I heard Ben tell her to believe in the tales, the Great Spirit always sends us help in time of need.

The people stood clear as the engine sparked to life. Dakota gave one last wave to her new family and accelerated down the rough strip. We wanted to see the area of the North Slope of the Brooks Range so swung North. Refueling at Wainwright and Barrow and Umiat. The country rose slightly in the direction of the Brooks Range. Rivers crossed our path. The weather remained good as we navigated toward the Haul Road from Fairbanks to Prudhoe Bay. We intersected the road as it crossed the range and flew South to home.

Chapter 15

Dakota's Surprise

It didn't take long for Dakota to have the magnificent bear hide laid out on the cabin floor. We sat at the table admiring the huge head and smooth thick fur. Dakota said that she thought it to be bigger than the mounted bear in the Fairbanks airport lobby. I had to agree. She still wondered about the burned hunter.

I looked forward to quiet time writing but Dakota had other ideas as she spread out the well worn map on the table. Pointing, she said "Look Paul, Anaktuvuk Pass is here and we are here. It looks like a short flight and I would like to see it. Want to go?" Like I said before, I wanted to write of our trip to Point Hope and didn't want to admit that I was tired. I hated the thought of not seeing her but told her that I felt that she was more than ready to cross country by her self. She seemed reluctant at first but had to agree that it was time.

The next day we serviced the Cub, packed the back with supplies and early the following morning she set out on her first solo cross country.

The cabin was now still as a tomb with only the occasional caw of a passing raven. On occasion I got up to pour a cup and once to throw open the old door to let in more summer air. The story of the Great White Bear and the dog flowed onto the paper, as I also wrote a companion story. Ben Bear Hunter had kept us all on the edge, as he told of the exploits of the Revenue Cutter Bear. He had unmeasured knowledge of the ship and crew as well as their many exploits. I especially liked the story of Capt Healey spending his own money in Siberia to bring Reindeer to mainland Alaska. Eventually this small group of animals grew into a vast heard, providing the people with food and a new found livelihood.

As I wrote, day flowed into evening and then into morning. I woke, finding myself still at the table. There, laying on the big rug,

I saw my two occasional companions. Paw to paw stretched out in unworried sleep. Hoping not to wake them, I slipped out the door to take care of morning business.

I built up the out side fire in the pit and had coffee boiling in the pot, by the time they lazily walked out the door. How I loved these two dogs. Pure beauty, clean, unruffled, as if they were in perfect being. Of course this in fact, is the state in which they dwelled. I gave up trying to understand it a long time ago. "Well my friends, how are you this fine morning?" Their only reply, an askant glance in unison. How I wished that they could talk. I went into the cabin to bring out fixings for breakfast, only to find them still setting in the same spot on my return. "Hungry?" Once again that glance. "Well lets fix us some grub." I fried a whole pound of bacon and enough fried potatoes, to surly satisfy all of us. I have heard that one is not supposed to feed dogs potatoes but have never had a problem with it. As I added the onions, Spirit wrinkled her nose. "Don't like onions girl?" I added the salt and pepper. At that, Spirit sneezed. " Bless you, if you don't like it don't eat it." Famished, I poured my cup full and sat out three equal shares. Before I had one bite finished their plates were empty. Broken Eye belched a good one. Spirit licked her lips and went for the skillet. Before I could say, hot, she jumped back with singed tongue. "That will teach you, should have learned the first time." Spirit circled the skillet a couple more times and after deciding that it was cool enough, licked it clean with Broken Eye's help. They then scampered off in search of who knows what. I felt blessed as two more days passed with writing, chores and long walks with the dogs. I felt that Dakota should have returned and began to be concerned for her. One thought or another passed before me, as I began to imagine all sorts of unpleasant things that could have happened to her. Then as we sat in the cabin finishing the evening meal, we heard that familiar sound. Spirit first, as her ears perked up, then Broken Eye. As we went to the door I hoped that the dogs would not pull their disappearing act, that Dakota would at last be able to meet them.

The Cub came in low and fast, bouncing at least three times before settling down to a stop. I ran for the door of the Cub wondering if perhaps Dakota was sick or something. She jumped out and flew into my arms. She could hardly contain her enthusiasm. "Paul, you would not believe it." I tried to draw her close but she drew back, pouring out her excitement. "I had the most fantastic trip of my life." We quickly grabbed her bags and walked toward the cabin. Dakota jabbering all the way. I wanted very much to hear every thing she had to say but at the same time hoped that the dogs hadn't disappeared. We went through the door, Dakota stopped in her tracks at the grin on Spirits face. The two dogs laid on their bellies, heads laying on the bears big head. They were stretched out full length, hind legs and tails behind them,

Once over her initial surprise, Dakota approached them cautiously. Spirit rolled over on her back for a belly scratch. Dakota honored her request, Broken Eye chimed in and nuzzled Dakota so vigorously, that all rolled together in a ball of laughter. All I could do was laugh and say "meet the dogs."

I fixed another supper for Dakota while she acquainted herself with her new friends. They would not let her out of their sight. I think they ate more than she did as Dakota fed them one for one. The meal ended and I cleaned up my mess. Making sure to clean the skillet before Dakota saw it. Dakota sat at the table, cup in one hand and a hand full of Spirit fur in the other, Dakota spoke. "You ready?" I sat down next to her and listened. "You would not believe how much I enjoyed my escapade. After I took off from here I circled once and headed West." I nodded in agreement as I was the one left behind and watched her go. "I crossed a low range of mountains just as the map showed. The Cub was running great and I maintained altitude, spotting the North Fork of the Koyukuk River a short time later. By the map I made a turn North, heading toward the North Fork of Ernie Creek. I started to get a little confused about then, as there was a cloud bank in my way." At that I asked "what did you do?" "just hush Paul and I'll tell you." I couldn't help but think of her blindly flying into some mountain. "I flew through it." "Flew through it?" I rolled my eyes as she went on. "It just happened to be a little cloud bank and I didn't think I would fly into any thing. I have to confess that I was wrong as I came out the other side and turned just in time." This girl was scaring me. "What do you mean turned just in time?" "Well there just happened to be a big white sheep standing on top of this mountain ." "A big white sheep? You mean a big Dall

Sheep?" "Yes Paul, a big white Dall Sheep." I must have not been too concerned, as I asked her if it had a full curl to it's horns. "I don't know Paul I hauled the Cub over just as I missed. "What do you mean just as you missed?" "Paul if you don't stop interrupting me, I am not going to tell you the story."

I shut my mouth, and got up and poured another cup, with the smallest amount of medicine in it. Just enough rum to cut my nerves. "Go on I'm ready." Dakota got up and went out side. I sat there for a long time wondering if I had hurt her feelings. On her return, she took up where she left off. I began to wonder if she was pulling Ben Bear Hunter's trick on me for the effect of the story. "The weather after that was perfect as I flew up the creek to Ernie Pass. At the top of the pass the mountains fell in a gradual slope. I passed over a small heard of caribou moving slowly in single file. What a sight they are to see." "How many where there?" "Paul I told you to stop interrupting me. There were only five or six." At once it crossed my mind of the vast herds that my father had told me about. Even I, when I was younger, saw a lot of big herds. Before my mind wandered too far into the glorious past, Dakota brought me back. "I followed the creek and came out into this wide area of rolling hills, spotting Anaktuvuk Pass. The village is small but beautiful laying South of the pass. I checked the empty strip and brought her in. I found a place out of the way and staked the Cub down. I had planed on spending the night under the wing but was shortly interrupted by visitors." "What kind of visitors?" "Paul, shut up." I knew that I had crossed the line and sat quietly as she continued. "A man and a woman suddenly were there. I didn't see them coming, I guess because I was busy unloading my stuff. Any way, he had on buckskins like you see in a movie and she had a great red blanket wrapped around her. Her long black hair flowed in the wind. They didn't say any thing at first, just looked at the plane. When I tried to introduce my self they interrupted me and said they knew my name. At first I didn't think any thing about it but then again I wondered how they could possibly know it."

Here we go again I thought, Dakota enters the spirit world and doesn't even know it. I decided that I had better keep my mouth shut, besides I wanted to see where this tale was going.

"They insisted that I stay with them and I accepted. We went up toward the village, sort of at the end of things. Their cabin was small, made of wood planks and covered with tar paper. Once inside, I couldn't believe my eyes. There were beautiful hides of fur every where. They were of many colors and descriptions. mink, otter, moose, bear, ermine, wolverine, wolf, and the list went on and on. Even though a cold breeze came off the pass the little place was warm and cozy.

The lady offered me some tea, which I readily accepted. She told me that she had never developed a taste for coffee. The man sat silent." I wanted to tell her that I thought I already knew who her new friends were but bit my tongue. Dakota went on. "The couple had very little in the way of home furnishings, just a cooking pot and kettle. Both hung over an open fire on iron rods. The fire place reminded me of pictures I had seen in some magazine. Sort of like the old days in Virginia or Kentucky. Oh yes, there were two bows with old looking arrows hung over the mantle. An another thing. The fire was made from logs and I wondered where they came from, as there were no trees in the area."

It became late and I could hardly keep my eyes open when Dakota stopped her story for the night. I looked down at the dogs and they each had one ear up, as though they waited for the story to go on.

We woke to the familiar sound of an engine in the distance. By the time we threw on our clothes, My sons Otter approached the end of the strip. We got out side just in time to see it swing around and the prop come to a stop. With our arms out stretched we greeted Ladonna and the twins. Boy how they were growing. I scooped both of them up in my arms as Ladonna and Dakota embraced and chattered like magpies. Both Spirit and Broken Eye came out the cabin door and about knocked Ladonna down in their excitement.

That evening we had a fine meal of turkey that Ladonna had brought up frozen, sweet potatoes, apple pie as well as a salad. It is always a treat when Ladonna brings up things that we ordinarily don't have to eat.

As the hours grew into late evening, Meg and Liz laid on the bear skin with Broken Eye and Spirit each watching over them. Every once and a while I caught one of the dogs giving the twins a big sloppy lick.

Earlier, I had warned Ladonna not to tell who she thought the couple were, that Dakota would tell about. Dakota backtracked on her story and brought Ladonna up to date. The cabin lay quiet while Dakota went on. "I still had no idea who these people were but wanted to be polite and did not push it. The woman suggested that I go to the clinic. She said that I would find it interesting. I asked her to come along but she said she would catch up with me later. I didn't go to the clinic right away but walked around the little village for a while. People that I saw were polite and I thought a little shy. They did not look like the woman who had befriended me. They were shorter and didn't have the same features as the woman in the red blanket. I saw the school and the store and the post office. There were snow machines out side of the houses but I didn't see many dogs. I had hoped that I would see lots of dogs." I wanted to tell her that the people of the North don't use dogs as much as they used to. They have given up a lot of the old ways, finding life softer with modern equipment. I wanted to tell her that I thought that this was sad. That some thing was lost in their embrace of modernism. I kept quiet for the time being, while my thoughts returned to Dakota's yarn.

"I eventually went to the clinic only to find it closed. I was about to turn around and leave when a short dark woman with a jolly voice gave a long H-e-l-l-o. She introduced her self as Noma. She opened the door and we went inside. The clinic was small by the standards I am used to but looked as though it was quite useful and clean. Noma told me that she was one of three Village Health Aides. Over a cup of coffee Noma told me that a few people would come in shortly. She just had time to ask me what I did and as I told her that I was a nurse, her first patient came in the door.

The man must have been seventy or so and complained of dizziness. Noma went through a very comprehensive history and as I watched she took his temperature, blood pressure, and had him open his shirt. He seemed drawn back as he looked in my direction, so I attempted to leave. Noma told the man that I was a nurse and he smiled a toothless grin and let her listen to his chest. After listening for a while she motioned for me to listen. Every thing seemed to be fine except for a few pops and crackles in the lungs and what sounded like a small murmur. I handed the stethoscope back to her as she looked at his chart. Noma asked him if he was taking his medicine and he admitted that he hadn't. She sat down with him and explained that the medicine should be taken that the doctor in Anchorage had started him on. After a while another patient came in. Noma reassured the old man that he would be ok and asked for him to come back in two weeks. The old man left and Noma greeted another person. Just then one of the other Village Health Aides came in and the day progressed with patients until the place was empty about ten AM.

Noma asked me if I wanted to come to her house to eat and I gladly accepted. The house was small, not much bigger than our cabin. When we went through the door we were greeted by two daughters. Lunch was on and the aroma filled my nostrils. Before I sat down I couldn't help but look into the pot on the stove. As I peered in Noma said that it was caribou stew. I turned toward the table and mentally tried to identify the contents of the pot. One of the girls ladled out a rather large portion, the second poured coffee. Forgetting my manners I started to eat just as Noma started the blessing. She began by thanking God for all that they had. Noma picked up a large loaf of freshly baked bread, blessed it, broke it and said take this in remembrance of our Lord. I was quite taken back and asked about it. She said that her family was one of a few Catholic families in the village. That a visit by a priest was so seldom that she used the prayer to teach her children about faith. As I thought about it, I ate as though I had never had a meal before. I must have been really hungry because I soon found myself on a second helping.

After the fantastic stew we sat around the table getting to know one another. She asked about my family and told me about hers. Her husband had died several years ago and she had help raising her daughters with help from all her relatives. We talked for a long time but mostly I listened. Noma said that her family had moved to the village when she was a young girl. They are known as Nunamiut, she went on to add that it means people of the land. They had always been nomads but had moved to the pass in three different bands in the late 1940's. The girls were getting a good education, both being in high school. They were not losing their language because the school had a teacher just for that purpose. I asked the girls what they wanted to do when they got out of school and both shyly giggled , saying that they wanted to go to Anchorage." I couldn't help but put in my opinion. "That's too bad, most young people cant wait to get to the big city. There they quickly loose their identity in the crowd."

I must have broken the spell of the story because Ladonna got up, yawned and put a blanket over the twins, saying that it was time for bed. By the time I came in from the out house everyone lay fast asleep.

I woke early the next morning finding Dakota at the table. I quietly slipped out, then returned, stopping at the stove to fill my cup before setting next to her. I sat there while she wrote feverishly. Finley she put her pen down and sighed. "You know Paul, I feel like I have been to the end of the earth." "I know what you mean." "Well that village is so beautiful, so wild, so remote. I hate to think of progress ever getting there, but it has." "Dakota, you should have seen this whole area when I was younger. The folks lived a hard life compared to what we have but they loved it. They were always so happy. Dad and mom, Charlie Two Bears, and the whole family struggled long distances to visit and hunt. They told so many stories, stories that I still recall to this day. I recall seeing my first airplane and never looked back. I had to fly. It's much like those two girls in Anaktuvuk Pass. We can only hope that they find their way in life and if their family is lucky, they will return and carry on."

We spent the rest of the day doing chores and playing with the twins. Ladonna took a long walk with the dogs. By evening we were ready to hear Dakotas story. Actually I could have spent the whole of the previous night listening to her. We all got good and comfortable around the table, as Ladonna and I each held one of the girls. The dogs seemed to be ready also, as they took up a good portion of the bear skin.

"Where was I?, oh yes. I spent a long time with Noma and the girls and then thanked them and returned to my hosts for the night. The cabin remained as I left it, the pot and kettle still on the fire. It appeared as though no one had moved, as though every thing remained suspended in time. Warmth exuded from the surroundings.

All remained quiet for a while then the woman spoke." "Did you have a good visit, see the village?" "Yes," then I told her of all that I had seen and done. The evening was quiet and I must have fallen asleep in the chair. I woke to find my hosts gone. I waited for ages for them to return but had to admit to myself that I needed to return home. I left a note thanking them for their hospitality, packed my bag and headed for the Cub.

I wanted one last look at the village and cabin, I had just left. I circled the village twice in disbelief, The first time I flew over the cabin, I didn't see it. The second time, a closer look convinced me that it should be there. Paul, The cabin was gone. The rest of the flight back was glorious with the weather perfect. I kept wondering if what I had seen or not seen meant anything. The mountain tops glistened and gave off an other world appearance. The water of Ernie Creek like a silver ribbon. I flew over the pass and startled a small heard of sheep grazing on the side of a mountain. Just after I crossed the pass, I looked out the left side and saw two people below walking next to the creek. As I passed over they turned and waved. A man and a woman. The woman wrapped in a red robe. Paul, I was miles from the village. No one could have walked that far, that fast."

I just grinned and gave a glance toward Ladonna. She was about ready to crack up. I could see that Ladonna had all she could do to contain herself. "Should I tell her?" Ladonna replied coyly and quietly, "I don't know, should you?" "Should you what?" Dakota came back. "Are you two playing a game with me, trying to mess up my mind?" I guess we were and it was fun. Just then, they appeared. First Paul then Rachael. They stood behind Dakota and both winked at us. Spirit game I thought. Dakota looked up at Ladonna and I and asked, "what?" "Turn around Dakota." She turned, I thought she would mess her drawers on the spot.

Chapter 16

A Gift for Dakota

We had a good laugh at Dakota's expense. Rachael took Dakota aside, just out of our hearing. Paul, my name sake, sat at the table. Paul in a hushed tone asked me how I was doing, as if he didn't know. We had a quiet conversation while Paul stroked Broken Eye's ear. Broken Eye sat with his head on Paul's lap. Spirit watched Rachael's every move, her tail wagging ever so slowly. Rachael motioned Ladonna over to the corner of the cabin and the three of them talked quietly.

Dakota made tea for Paul and Rachael which they seemed to relish. Finally Paul got up and motioned Dakota to the corner. How I wished to hear that conversation. It seemed as though they were there one minute and gone the next. The room had a warm glow to it as Dakota wept. There seemed nothing that I could do or say that would stop her tears.

The next morning found the dogs gone also. The rug empty and seemingly very big with out them laying on it. The mood around the old place changed, or appeared to change, as good byes were said and Ladonna and the girls took off the end of our little strip.

Once again we were alone. Dakota appeared to be very calm and I actually thought that I heard her humming as I fixed breakfast. "You in better spirits today?" "Yes Paul, sorry about last night. I actually was very happy, the tears were of joy. Rachael and Paul both had words for me. Rachael explained who they were and their relation to the family. She welcomed me to the clan with open arms. Rachael talked to me about faith and action. She explained why her and Paul popped into our lives every so often. She told me that the Lord loves me and that all I have to do is believe. Paul told me that my first husband did not die in vein and that he was at peace now. I had not realized that I carried so much pain in my heart. He touched me with the touch of an Angel and all the hurt went away. I am at peace for the first time in memory."

I had been thinking of a surprise for Dakota and going to Fairbanks held the answer. "Would you like some time alone?" "Yes Paul." I then told her of my desire to get away for a while. We spent the rest of the day in quiet company and the next day I took off. I missed Dakota deeply even before I got to the Yukon River. By the time I circled Fairbanks I wanted to return.

The kids greeted me warmly after I taxied to the hanger. It was good to be back but my heart remained at the cabin. Lunch, a specialty of Joe's, was great. I suppose he always fancied himself as a Dagwood, piling sandwiches high with every thing he could find in the refrigerator.

Joe did not look well, he seemed slow at every thing he did or said. He still could not get medical clearance to return to the air. I hoped for the best for him but had my doubts. Ladonna and her younger brother called me aside later and gave me the news. The doctors felt that Joe would never improve. They told the kids that the head injury would never get any better, feeling that he had gone too long without treatment.

That evening I still mulled over my sons condition and prayed for an answer. It is with deep sadness, that we have to face turmoil in the lives of our children. I grabbed onto the belief that God would give Joe healing.

While we sat around the table after supper I mentioned my idea. "I want to find an airplane for Dakota." I had thought I might find resistance from the kids but they jumped at the thought. They started talking at once but deferred to Joe as he spoke slowly. "I, know, where, there, is, a, good, one, dad." Tears welled up from the bottom of my heart to hear Joe speak. Right then and there I made a resolution to bombard the gates of Heaven for him. "Whatcha got son?" I had to turn away so he could not see the tears streaming down my face. "I'll, show, you, tomorrow, it's, a, Cessna."

We broke for the night, I could not take any more. The night passed through the long hours as I petitioned my Lord in every way possible. I wrestled with my pillow for sleep. Finally I got up and went to the kitchen. Ladonna sat in the dark, on one of the stools at the counter. With out a word, I turned on a small light and went to the cupboard and pulled out a cup. As I sat across from her, I about burned my mouth sipping the hot coffee. Ladonna grinned and spoke. "Just what I needed dad, a good chuckle."

After I got over the burn, I said "glad to help you out." We talked until morning, I being happy to have such a daughter. We argue from time to time but the love between us is strong.

Dave came by and grabbed some breakfast, before greeting some fishermen he had scheduled to fly out. Joe showed up around ten and took me out to the airport. We stopped in front of a hanger that I was vaguely familiar with. I hadn't been to this end of the strip in years. The old hanger looked as though it would collapse at any moment. It should, because it was old when I learned to fly. Joe still had his usual strength, sliding the old doors aside easily. The plane stood alone, covered with a dusty tarp.

I couldn't wait to take off the tarp as Joe spoke. " I, think, it, is, a, Cessna, 172 B, from, about, 1960, or, so." She actually was covered by three old tarp's. We each uncovered a wing and then The fuselage. I stood back. She appeared to be as clean as a whistle. "An, old, lady, owns, it." Joe said, he knew the owner and the old widows plane hadn't flown in years. I knew that I wanted it and asked Joe for the phone number.

I hired a mechanic to help us get her back in the air. We took the wings off and hauled her back to our hanger. Once at home we spent days going over every inch of the Skyhawk. Joe had not lost his mechanical ability but about drove us nuts with his slow speech. I wanted desperately to see Dakota and her reaction to her new bird. Besides I wanted my Cub back.

Finally the day arrived to take her up in her new life. Ladonna sat next to me at the duel controls. There were more gauges than I could count. My Cub is a simple plane and just the way I like it. I suppose if I had learned to fly in a biplane, I still would. Kind of old fashioned I guess. With Ladonna in the right seat, I fired her up. The blue smoke rolled out of the new engine, as she coughed a few times and settled into her rhythm. With all the pre flight checks done and the engine purring like a kitten, we rolled down the strip. She lifted into the air as though she had been waiting especially for this day. We flew out over the Tannana River toward Nenanna, catching a view of Mt Denali and the Alaska Range. Ladonna took the controls for a time and put the Cessna through her paces. I knew that Dakota would love her new friend.

Winter would not be a long time coming and we packed the Cessna for my return journey. We found a new set of skis that we strapped to the undercarriage. She had ample room in the cabin for all the things that Dakota and I would need for a long winter. On a cool September morning we sat at the table for breakfast. The kids would fly up in a few weeks with more supplies as well as to return my Cub. Good byes were said and at the last minute Ladonna handed me a gift.

What a little fur ball, one, perhaps two pounds, at the most. "What is this?" "Well dad, It looks like a dog to me" Ladonna replied. "What in the heck am I supposed to do with it?" I held it up in front of me for a better look. "Well dad I suppose you will love it for one thing." Ladonna replied.

It sat on the seat next to me while I prepared to taxi. "You just stay put and don't get caught in the controls and no funny business." I said, then we took off. Once airborne I looked over at the fur ball. He sat up on his haunches, reminding me of a little prairie dog looking out of his burrow. Kind of a cute little thing I thought. "Well I don't know what good you will be but we will see."

Dakota jumped up and down with excitement when I handed her the keys to her Cessna. She ran around it, sat in the cockpit and ran her hands over every surface. I never knew that I could create such joy from a gift. "Aren't you glad to see me?" "Of course Paul, one thing at a time." Hugs and kisses abounded. One more surprise for Dakota as we went toward the cabin. Once inside I took the pup out of my jacket and sat him on the bear skin rug. He promptly peed on it. Dakota scooped him up as I went for a rag. "How cute." She held him in the air, "A little boy, what's your name?"

Dakota finally put the dog down long enough to ask me if I was hungry. "I'm famished." I said, as I told her that I would cook supper after we unloaded the new plane. "No you don't, you have done enough for one day." The meal was good but the loving better.

Chapter 17

Thanksgiving and the Clan

Dakota poured over the manual for the Cessna all morning. About noon we took off. I sat in the right seat and Dakota blasted down the strip and into the air. The new dog sat on my lap, occasionally standing to look out the right window. We flew in clear skies until the fuel ran low then returned to the cabin.

I knew she was more than delighted as she kept telling me how much she liked each little thing about the Cessna. "What you going to name your bird?" I said over coffee. "Well it is a Skyhawk, so I guess it's name will be Hawk." I came back with another question. "What you going to name the dog?" "What do you mean the dog. This is not just the dog", as she took him from my lap and sat him on the table. I had to reply "dog on the table?" "Hush Paul, it can't be any worse than the way you don't clean the skillet." "OK, OK girl, I get the point." He sat on the table in front of Dakota, looking at her with those little black eyes. His fur a light tan in color and tiny pink tongue just protruding from his partially open mouth. He waged his tail feverishly while she stroked his fur. It was obvious that he was never going to be a big dog, I doubt not much more than eight or ten pounds full grown. I could see Dakota struggling for a name, as I got up to refill the cups. She took him in her arms and cradled him like a baby. "Tuk, that's your name!"

Thanksgiving morning broke with new fallen snow blanketing everything. I came in from my morning chores and looked in at Dakota and Tuk curled up in a ball, still sleeping. Tuk had taken right away to sleeping between us. I rebelled but to no avail. He said that it was his place and no one could dislodge him from it. After a few nights I quit trying. The mornings were cold now and the old stove made its usual chugging sound as the new wood caught fire. The coffee boiled on the stove, much as coffee had boiled on it for all the years the McAuffe's had occupied the place. While I waited for the grounds to settle I contemplated the new day. I watched the pup as he poked his head out of the covers once, than decided to go back to sleep. A new sound jarred me from my thoughts. Off in the distance at first, then closer and louder. We weren't expecting any company and had decided not to do anything special on this day. I went to the window only to see not one but two aircraft, setting up to land. I gently shook Dakota and told her that we had company. I threw on my parka and went to greet the visitors. While they landed one after another I knew this would turn out to be a special day. No sooner had the first plane taxied in and shut down than the second did the same.

Ladonna, Al, the twins, Ian, Ian's friend, Dave, Joe, Joe's friend, three of Ladonna's friends, and last but not least Fr Paddy. I stuck my head into the door of the second Otter, to see if any one else would come out. Where would we put them all? They all paraded to the cabin carrying bundles of gear. I wondered how we would feed them on such short notice. I had taken out one moose roast from the cache just thirty minutes before.

I squeezed myself into the cabin only to see a pile of coats on the bed as well as mounds of sleeping bags. On the table, stacked high were the fixings for one gigantic Thanksgiving dinner. All talked at one time and these old ears had a hard time deciphering one conversation from another.

Ian was the first to slap me on the back with a mighty blow and grip my hand in a painful vise. I thought to myself that I should have been more on guard. He introduced his friend. "Well lad, this is Peggy!" I was bowled over by this raving beauty with long red hair. "Where might I ask did an ugly Scott as yourself find such a charming lass?" Ian roared with laughter,"Edinburgh, lad, Edinburgh." Ian started to tell me the tale of their meeting but promptly interrupting me, Joe introduced Caroline. "Dad, this, is, my, friend, Caroline, I, hope, that, you, don't, mind, my, bringing, her." Hell, I thought, trying to keep the tears from my voice. Joe had never found any one before and I sure as hell was glad to meet her. "Mr. McAuffe, I am so glad to meet you." I put my arms around her, held her close and whispered "I am dad." I knew the instant and it must have been some kind of revelation, that this girl was a future daughter in law.

I felt something jumping up and down on my leg. I looked down knowing that Tuk was lost in a sea of legs. "Come on up squirt" as I bent to lift him. About that time Fr. Paddy came my way through the crowd. "Are you ready lad?" "Ready for what father?" I said through the din of the room. Just then Caroline grabbed his arm and escorted him away. I elbowed my way over to the stove, in time to hear Dakota ask me to open the door, as it was getting too hot in there. I threw the door part way open only to see Dave covering the wings of the Otters, while the snow began to fall again. The women were busy preparing the meal and chattering away. I grabbed my cup and put a wee tad of spirits in it, just to keep me steady of course. Tuk peered out of my arms not knowing what to make of all the people. I asked where the twins were only to find them in the arms of Ladonna's friends as they stirred something on the stove. Ian engaged his woman in serious conversation in the corner.

About the time the great Turkey went in the oven, Fr. Paddy made an announcement. "My brothers and sisters, I have the privilege of announcing the wedding of our friends Joseph and Caroline." The room fell silent. I most of all. The shock reverberated through to my bones. If this wasn't enough he announced that the wedding would take place immediately. Joe and Caroline looked in my direction as tho looking for my blessing. All I could manage was a smile.

The ceremony lasted only ten or so minutes, shortest Catholic wedding I could imagine. The couple embraced ,as the crowd roared with applause, then broke into merriment all around. I could not get close to the newlyweds but managed to side up to Dakota. "Did you know anything about this?" "I just found out about an hour ago Paul, they wanted it to be a surprise." I squeezed her waist and said "I guess so!"

We had to eat in shifts because there was not enough room at the table. People helped them selves to turkey, dressing, potatoes both sweet and white, greens, apple sauce and a whole gambit of foods I could not identify or recall. The wine flowed to the point that I thought we would run out. I didn't want Fr, Paddy to have to try and turn water into wine. I don't know though, I couldn't help but wonder where all the wine was coming from. Tuk begged from every one in the place. As I was finally able to set next to the newlyweds, I amazed at the amount of food that we had consumed. As people became full, the room fell to a quieter level. At that, Fr. Paddy asked the blessing. "Children, I suppose you wonder why the blessing is being asked after we eat. Well its both a blessing and a giving of thanks. Besides I have your undivided attention." A chuckle ran through the room. He raised his hands toward heaven and said, "We thank you Father for all that we have. We thank you for wonderful friends, hospitality, health, well being, and this fine meal made by the hands of Earthly Angels. We also ask that you bless this couple on their day. The day they start on a road known only by you. Bless both of you and bless you all." The room remained silent for a second ,then erupted in cheers and the raising of glasses in a toast. Ian raised his glass high and furthered the thoughts of Fr. Paddy, then announced his up coming wedding to the beautiful Peggy.

There's something about a large gathering of clan that grips the soul. Families large and small touch one another in ways that God only knows. A kind word here, a hug there and on occasion, a soon forgotten harsh engagement of words. Our family was no different. Pranks and stories finally dribbled away about midnight. Dave had strung two hammocks in the far corner over an old sea chest. We installed old Fr. Paddy in the lower one and I cant recall who in the upper. Several or more people spread out sleeping bags on the big bear. All in all it's amazing that all found a place for the night. In the last moments of wakefulness, I thought I heard the quiet sounds of marriage consummation.

I don't know who awoke first but I could smell the sweet aroma of my favorite morning coffee. One by one all got up, with some meekly holding their heads. Peggy, who I had not yet been able to acquaint my self, had breakfast well in hand. She seemed quite capable of orchestrating the others in the fine art of putting breakfast on the table. Little did I know at the time, that she worked every day as head chef at a five star hotel in Edinburgh. It was a surprise to me that Fr.Paddy didn't say Mass, only a blessing and reminder for all to fare well.

We watched while Dave's Otter left plumes of new fallen snow as he charged off the strip. All that remained of the group, Ian and Peggy, Al and Ladonna, the twins, and Dakota and I, hastily went back into the cabin. Every one had fairly well cleaned up their mess so we finished the job. As I picked up something I glanced toward Peggy. God was she a good looking woman. I had to remind myself that Dakota remained all that I could handle.

Ten in the morning and I had to take a nap. Tuk quickly snuggled under the covers as every one else wound down also. Noon again found us eating. Peggy put together quite a spread out of who knows what. Fanciest food the old cabin ever saw.

Peggy and I finally had time to get acquainted. Ian did most of the acquainting. I still had a hard time getting used to this guy. Or perhaps I had a touch of jealousy over his accomplishment. I had to think about that one. They met as he took his holiday away from the remote arctic weather station. Apparently it had been love at first sight and they did not take a lot of time deciding that they were meant for each other. I thought perhaps he knew a good cook when he saw one.

Al had finished his stint on Banks Island and planned on writing a paper on the musk ox as well as the Native Peoples. Ladonna wanted to return to work, because Dave had been overwhelmed with the business. Since Joe could no longer fly, it had fallen to Dave to hold things together. Ladonna had helped as she could, but the children required most of her time. Al had the perfect suggestion and Ladonna jumped at it. He would become a house dad. Al said that he could write and get reacquainted with his girls.

It appeared that every one had every thing figured out and what could I add. Even though I loved them all dearly I really wanted some peace and quiet.

Chapter 18

An Arctic Christmas

Christmas approached while Dakota and I lived each day as it came. The days were short and the nights long. The temperature outside hovered around 50 below, plus or minus a couple of degrees. In our cabin we delighted in the heat from the stove. Tuk grew to the gigantic size of four pounds in the couple of months we had him. He spent a great deal of time in the wood box next to the stove. Try as I may, I could not dislodge him. I made a special box for him but gave up and used it for the wood. When he wasn't laying in our laps he curled up in the bottom of his wood box. Occasionally we would see a little head, black nose and two little eyes staring at us. When ever we ate, he had to eat also. Tuk mastered the fine art of begging. We thought of his health of course but turning down Tuk when he begged remained difficult. He worked our hearts.

Every evening I carved on a piece of moose antler. I tried to keep Dakota from seeing it as it was supposed to be a Christmas present. As I worked on it I thought back to the Christmas in the 1600's, that my namesake Paul carved the items for his family. It was just a small piece that I delicately carved. Each line took on the character of the work my grandfather did so well. Old sailors carved ships and whales and many other items that they were familiar with. I had to be different. I carved a Cessna on ski's as the main figure. As I worked I had to decide just what its use would to be. It was decided for me when a piece broke off in my hand, almost taking my thumb with it. It would be a broach or perhaps a necklace if I could find an old gold chain. I got up and looked next to the shaving mirror. There it hung. The chain had belonged to my mother, long since gone, the item that it held. With a finishing touch, I cut a shallow place and glued in a gold nugget. I thought it rather beautiful.

Tuk's gift proved to be more difficult. I thought for the better part of a week, before I came up with the winning idea. Since he loved to chew on everything in sight, I decided on dog biscuits and chews. As I worked Dakota spoke, "what in the word are you doing this time of day, messing in the kitchen?" "Quiet, I can't answer out loud, that dog understands every thing I say and I don't want to spoil the surprise." I experimented with all kinds of mixes, finally settling on dried caribou and salmon mixed with flour and water. I mixed in a little salt and formed little dog treats just big enough for his little jaws. I baked them hard as a rock, thinking that ought to keep him busy for a while. I also cut strips of jerky and wrapped them in pieces of old newspaper.

I also had another project. Dakota about had a fit when one day I brought an old engine into the cabin. When the kids were younger we had an old snow machine, one of the first ones made. It had long since died but I got the idea that perhaps I could make it come back to life. I have no idea where I got the bright idea because I didn't like the dam noisy thing when it was new.

The first thing I did was to spill the oil all over the floor which Tuk just had to walk in. Dakota about died with that. I cleaned the dog and the floor. Actually the floor hadn't shined like that since I spilled the engine oil on it and the table from the bucket.

Long hours were spent taking that piece of crap apart, checking each item and reassembling it. It looked like new when I finished. I never did find any thing wrong with it. I even had parts left over. I dreaded going back out side and reinstalling it back where it came from. However this is what I did. I about froze my fingers in the process but after cleaning out the gas tank and refilling it, the moment of truth arrived. Dakota with Tuk peeking out of her Parka watched as I pulled the rope. Nothing happened. I pulled again and fiddled with the carb. Nothing. A little more adjustment and pull again. Dakota about had enough, she turned to go, just as the engine caught. About time I thought, while it slowly crept forward. The engine whined wide open as the rust cracked on the boggy wheels and the track made its first turn in years. All of a sudden every thing broke loose and I about fell off the back. She leaped down the run way, while I congratulated my self at the never before attained speed. I soon realized the throttle had stuck wide open. I ran out of runway and leaped off, tumbling into the snow head first. By the time I got up and brushed the snow out of my eyes the machine sat at the end of the runway idling. I promptly got on, hit the gas and sped back to Dakota. "Want a ride?" "No but no thanks, you wont catch me on that thing." We'll see I thought as I had one more idea up my sleeve.

I rummaged around the rafters of our old hanger. There, way back from the ladder, lay one of my mom's old dog sleds. After crawling through who knows what I found it and brought it down tug by tug. There was no telling the age on this one. Covered in years of dust and showing signs of gnawing by porcupines I thought it could be repaired. After about two days of work in the hanger I managed to put her back together. In addition I built a tongue to attach to the snow machine. I next took two moose hide robes from the cabin.

It took some tall convincing but Dakota and Tuk sat in the basket of the sled. I looked back to see Tuk just peering out of Dakota's parka ruff. Throttle to the wall we were off. I took it easy on them at first. My mothers sled trails of the past were not as good as the old days. Up one hill and down another we flew. I could hear screams of delight in back of me. Finally after about five miles I stopped. Dakota threw open the robes and jumped out. Tuk grinned from ear to ear. Dakota laughed with abandon. Her face and parka hood covered with packed snow. She shouted "get in" as she handed Tuk in my direction. I don't know if it was an act of vengeance or sheer joy but she drove like a bat out of hell back to the cabin. I had to laugh as I threw open the robe and Tuk and I got out. I couldn't help but say "I'll bet my mother never went that fast on that sled." Dakota made a snow ball and hit me square in the forehead. The fight erupted as we warred with snow balls all the way to the cabin door.

Christmas eve saw us walking out to the end of our strip. Snow crunched under our feet. The temperature had gone up in the last few days. It now hovered at twenty below. The sky laid out stars by the thousands. The universe lay before us as Northern Lights played all the way down to the cabin. They danced so close we felt as though we could touch them. "Look Tuk your first shooting star." Tuk appeared not to be impressed. We stood arm in arm for a long time drinking in the sights of God.

Once inside, I stoked the fire and put on the old pot to boil. The aroma of fresh baked goods filled the air. After I stuffed my face, I handed Dakota her gift. Her face lit up as she opened it. "It's beautiful Paul, put it on me." She continued to admire it while I reached around her to latch the chain. Tuk sat on the table. I handed the small news paper wrap to him and watched him tear it open. He held it with his paws first one way than another. Finally he had his prize. He bit down hard and spit it out. "Hey man, that's good, I made them for you." I wondered what I did wrong only to notice Dakota holding a cookie out for him just out of my vision. She cracked up.

"Here Paul, Merry Christmas." The box was small, and flat. I slowly opened it. A hand knitted wool scarf. One big enough to keep me warm. "You make this?" "Yes Paul, some times you don't pay any attention to me, so it was easy to keep it from you." I had to think about that as I always think that I pay too much attention to Dakota. "I love it, just what I've always wanted." She looked hurt. "Really girl, I haven't had one of these since I was a kid." I still think that I didn't convince her.

Dakota pulled out an envelope. "How about this? Perhaps this is better." I opened it and found two tickets to Scotland. My eyes about popped out. "Wow are we really going to the wedding?" "Looks like it dear, unless you don't want to go." I picked her up and swung her about the room.

I thought the excitement of the gift exchange over but I thought too soon. I dropped Dakota to her feet I turned around. Laying on the white rug, Broken Eye and Spirit, at the table, Paul and Rachael. "Merry Christmas." "And a Merry Christmas to you" I came back. One would think I would get used to spirits dropping in at any old time but I never did.

Paul handed me a beautiful hand made bow with arrows. Not the kind you buy at the sporting goods store but real hand made and right out of the past. Rachael let Dakota unwrap her gift. One really magnificent red blanket to match hers. We were with out words as we accepted these gifts. Rachael told Dakota that she thought she might like a red blanket as much as she always had. Dakota wiped away tears of joy and I just sat there dumbfounded.

"I'm forgetting my manners"as Dakota went to the stove. "Let me help", Rachael said. In no time I had a fresh cup of coffee and Dakota, Paul and Rachael steaming mugs of black tea.

"We could not help but notice how you and Dakota marveled over God's handiwork." Paul noted, "We watched you as the Northern Lights played with your emotions." Rachael replied "that last little display at the steps of the cabin was our handiwork, God lets us play on occasion also."

The three dogs seemed to enjoy each other' s company as Spirit and Broken Eye stretched out on the bear skin. Tuk looked dwarfed as he played between the two. Two hundred pounds of dogs with a four pound mut chewing on their ears. Tuk first scrambled over one then the other. Their patience mesmerized me.

Paul first to speak, asked if we understood the meaning of Christmas. I at first thought this a ridiculous question. Of course I understood. I interjected "Gifts were given in order to show love." " True but no cigar." "No cigar, what kind of talk is that coming from a spirit?" Paul continued, " I speak in words that you can understand." He went on,"Over the centuries man evolved in his thinking ability to the point where he needed more than what he had. He was not yet able to put into practice what he had already been taught. Moses and the Prophets had told them again and again what they must do and how they must live. The time had come for God to fulfill his promise to give man a redeemer. He chose to come to man as a child and a poor one at that. It is up to man to figure out the meaning of this action. Some people get it and some people don't." Just when I had a question ready to ask, they all disappeared.

Tuk, dwarfed by the big rug looked as though he had lost his best friends. I guess he had, I shook my head in shock, that they would bring up such a profound subject and then drop it in my lap and leave. "What in the world was that?" Dakota smiled and said, "That I guess was meant to make us think." "Dakota, I believe I have enough to think about with out going into some deep mystery." "It's not a deep mystery at all Paul, do think about it."

I wrestled with Paul's words all night and awoke from thought to the smell of bacon sizzling in the skillet and the never forgotten aroma of strong fresh coffee. "Breakfast" Dakota's voice ever so sweet brought me fully awake. "Hurry up Paul." "What's the hurry?" "Fresh snow and we need to go outside, come on, its Christmas morning."

We quickly ate and as I put on my gear, I rubbed the frost from the window. The thermometer said ten below. "Regular heat wave" I replied. Out the door we went, the new fallen snow took me by surprise. "Lets fly today Paul." I quickly warmed to the idea. I have flown many times in much colder weather but this day appeared perfect.

It took about three hours to clean off the snow of the previous night, heat the engine, put in the warm oil and generally prepare the Cessna. She was slow to turn over but caught. Blue smoke cleared away as the engine warmed. I freed the ski's from their frozen position and soon we slid down the strip. Once in the air Dakota took a hard bank to the right and we could still see the plume of new snow from our take off. Smoke lazily curled from our chimney. Tuk watched from his perch inside my parka, while we flew over the river and headed out over the tundra. What a beautiful morning. The dim winter light played smokey shadows over all below. Off to the South the dim light of the winter sun could just be made out, from our altitude.

Chapter 19

Back to the Island

The following spring found us high over Scotland. In the final hour of flight, I thought back over the centuries and our rich family heritage. The tales told of long ago brought forth images of John and Ootah, Lloyd and Angelene, the Wandering Priest and a whole host of people in our lineage. I must have day dreamed about them for a long time as Dakota had to wake me to prepare to land. We came in wide on our approach to Edinburgh and I felt as though part of me was coming home. I looked out the window and could imagine Lloyd looking for his bride.

Ian and Peggy met us at the terminal. This time I prepared myself for Ian's usual back slapping and crushing handshake. It didn't happen. He embraced me as a long lost brother. After we picked up our luggage and were about to enter the car, Ian caught me off guard ,as I fell forward under the weight of his mighty blow to my back. "Now lad you didn't think you would get away without a proper greeting, did you?" One of these days I thought, I'll get even with him.

In the week leading up to the wedding, Dakota made the rounds of all the shops the fine city had to offer. Peggy and Dakota shopped in a never ending affair. As much as I wanted to go to the wedding, I could not wait for the side trip to Colonsay, the ancestral home of my family. For the time being, Ian and I made the rounds of every pub in the city. It seems that Ian knew every one and we ended up buying pint for pint all over town. I don't mind a little rum in my coffee on occasion but some one ended up dragging me home every night.

Ladonna and Al left the twins with Joe and Caroline and joined us just in time for the wedding rehearsal. That went fine and the dinner was catered by Peggy's staff. What an event that was. Her chefs left no stone unturned in the preparation of everything that Scotland had to offer. By the time the pastry chef brought out her creation I had all I could do to put it away.

The wedding was held in a little stone church that had seen many centuries. I had the distinct feeling that spirits looked on at every turn. Finally much to my relief the party was over and the new bride and groom were off.

"Now can we go to Colensay?" "Yes Paul, now we can go to Colonsay." The rented car was small by any of my standards. We packed Al and Ladonna's suitcases as well as our own in and the four of us took off. Al did the driving, being used to the traffic and signs. All seemed strange. We passed place after place that touched my heart as though I had been there before.

After staying at several inns and seeing enough sights to last a life time, we finally caught the ferry to the island. Dakota had made arrangements for us to stay in a little cottage while the owners were away on holiday.

The following morning I got up before anyone else to see the sights. There was really not to much to see. The island is barren for the most part, rolling hills and an occasional pond. Cottages here and buildings of some use there. Ancient trees hold to life. The object of my search was not too hard to find.

The Standing Stone. Perhaps not the same stone but close enough. Malcom the last chief of the Macdubhsith Clan was tied to this rock in 1623 and executed. From that day on our family has been a broken clan. Scattering far and wide, they all have names that mean the same but are spelled differently. The list is long but a few are Coffey, Guffey, Phee, Phi, Mac Duffy, MacAuffy and many other sur name spellings.

The smell of the sea surrounded me in the cool morning air. I could close my eyes and almost touch the people. The bond remains over the centuries. Blood is blood as my father always said. I had no idea what he was talking about until that day, I touched the rock. I had come home, a full circle, so to speak. All the members of my clan spoke in my heart on that morning. I knew the stories to be true. Whatever their station in life, they were all my family.

It seemed like only minutes that I stood there but when I looked at my watch, hours had passed. I had felt as though I had left this Earth only to find home. I felt as though I had made a long journey and it was OK, every thing was OK.

I caught up with the others, that evening, had a small meal and went to bed. I could hear Ladonna ask Dakota if I was alright but never heard her reply as I drifted off to sleep. The most restful sleep in years.

Ladonna asked me to show her the rock on the next day but I declined. I feared that if I returned, the magic of the prior day would vanish. She told me of her initial disappointment but later she privately told me much the same story as I had experienced.

By the time the visit to Colonsay came to an end, I was at once ready and reluctant. The broader meanings of my heritage touched my soul. But leave we did and none too soon as Ladonna and Al longed to see their twins and Dakota and I needed the quiet of our Arctic cabin.

We arrived in Fairbanks as the sun still shined brightly. After two days catching up with needed chores, we flew on to our real home. Tuk who had stayed in Fairbanks , had been all over us and happy to see us. He still would not leave my lap and constantly looked at Dakota as if to say, don't leave me.

Chapter 20

Trouble With The Law

We were all glad for the peace and quiet of the North. The smells and sounds were familiar. The sky bluer and the whispers of the breeze danced to their own tune. I could not wait to spend my days writing. Dakota poured over her shopping treasures. She had purchased so much in Edinburgh, as well as every other stop, that I wondered where it would fit. Never underestimate the power of a woman to have everything in order before you can blink an eye. One minute it laid all over the cabin and the next it was gone. How do they do it?

Sounds of Pipers ran through my mind as Tuk sat in my lap while I attempted to write. For once I hoped that Dakota had traveling out of her system. I interrupted my writing and told the story of Gray Friars Bobby to Tuk. He listened to my every word and seemed to enjoy it. Contented, he turned two or three times and settled into a contented nap. With this, I started the novel "Five Pipers".

With the whole summer ahead of us, we hoped to accomplish a whole list of to do's. One to continue writing and others to get in some fishing and some time in archeological searches. Ladonna and Al, with the twins had planed to spend a month with us digging at a site in the Gates of the Arctic National Park.

There are many sites of interest with in the park boundaries and Al working thru the university wanted to look at one of them in particular. We all camped at a site that looked promising. What intrigued me most was the possibility of some fine fishing. I had little interest in digging holes in the ground for the fun of it. I had agreed to help the kids sift for artifacts. Dakota contented herself with the twins. The site sat next to a very small lake, no more than thirty by sixty feet. As usual it was crystal clear to the bottom. As at my former crash site, I could see that it would once again take class to catch fish.

I had thought that I would never eat another fish but once a fisherman always a fisherman.

I had never seen Al so excited. Apparently this was to be a first class site. He explained that there was much to do and it would take him forever to write every thing up.

I went fishing and no sooner wet a line than I heard this commotion from Al. "Yea, wahoo, look at this, come on, hurry." I could no more see a reason to hurry over a hole in the ground than the man in the moon. "Paul, Ladonna, Dakota, come on." My only reply was "shut up your scaring the fish." Dakota was the first to Al's side, then Ladonna. "Come on Paul you got to see this." By that time any thought of fish was out the window. "Hold your pants on, I'll be there in a minute."

Al fondly held and looked at what any idiot could call a perfect specimen of a bowl. My reply as I could feel Al's excitement was, "looks like a bowl to me." "Not any bowl Paul, but a bowl straight out of somewhere in Mongolia or Siberia." "How do you know that?" I replied. Al held it up to the light and caressed it like it was a gorgeous woman. "Well my friends this Bowl is at least 5000 years old. We'll know more, when it's carbon dated. You never find one so intact. Usually they are in fine bits and need to be carefully reconstructed. In addition to this, look there are bits and pieces indicating that this site was used continually up to about 500 years ago."

As I held the bowl something deep within my being changed. I could almost feel a presence of past owners. Al went on, "you know Paul, you talk all the time about your family history and this story and that story. These bits and pieces and this fine bowl are stories and tales of long ago and far off lands. They are as much stories as any you can tell."

I had to admit that he was more than likely right. I began to look at this site as something more. I started to scratch around, Al lowered the boom on me. "Come on Paul that's not the way to research a site properly. There has been and continues to be more destruction of antiquities by amateur diggers than you would believe." I sort of jumped back at that, then Al said, "Here let me show you what we need to do."

Now I knew why Al had taken so long before he dug the first earth. I now recalled him carefully mapping the site and laying down grids. He labeled each grid on his corresponding notes. He had looked at the site from every angle. If I would have been more interested in what he was doing instead of fishing I would have learned more.

"Ok Paul you see this grid where I dug the bowl?" I looked at it but Al apparently was not satisfied. "No Paul sit here for a while and look at it. What is it telling you? What is the story that is unfolding? What are you going to disturb and what are you going to get rid of? Here, see this?" I took a more careful look. Just jutting from the place where he had removed the bowl, there appeared to be a point of stone. "Here Paul take this brush and carefully remove the soil from around it." As I ever so carefully removed the soil from around it I could see what appeared to be a spear point. "Paul, before you lift it from the area, sift the soil you dug for more." I soon not only had my first spear point but from the sifting found small pieces of bone, pottery, shells and fine beads with holes in them.

Work for the day ended when supper was called. Al gave us quite a lecture that evening and I had a new found interest. I couldn't wait until the next day to be at it again. Ladonna did the cataloging as Al and I combed over more and more of the dig. I soon lost all interest in fishing.

The next day I practically tripped over an old tin can. I knew that Al must have not seen it because he would have picked it up and discarded it. I quietly put it in my coat pocket. I had an idea where the can came from. Later when Al wasn't looking I placed the can just under the surface of the ground next to my dig. When all was quiet and Al engrossed in his activities, I started hollering. "Al, Ladonna, Dakota, yahoo, wow, look at this. I found the mother load." They all came running. I just brushed off the last of the soil from the can as they arrived. "Look Al". He and the others looked at me as though I was stupid. "Look, evidence, that this site has been occupied in the last hundred years." I took out my trusty can opener and opened the can. "Military C rations, Mothers Cookies, still in perfect condition, some GI, has been here on a hunting trip." I couldn't help my self as I busted a gut laughing. I thought my humor quite outstanding, too bad others didn't share it.

At lunch I dunked my find of Mothers Cookies in my coffee. Quite good actually, no telling how old they were. "Well Al, don't you think we should have these carbon dated?" "Paul, I'm going to have you carbon dated."

All in all, the site proved to be a good one. It had been occupied by Yupik and Inupiat peoples. It was part of the small tool tradition as well as the artifacts that pushed the site even further back in time. The University would have to sort it all out.

Over the next weeks we continued to dig and catalog. Al had a treasure, a large one, to take back to the university. I for one enjoyed the project but started to long for home. At the end of the month we did just that. We were torn between wanting to stay with the twins and the peace of home.

Home won out and a new chapter to our lives began. While on final approach to our cabin, We could see that we had visitors. Setting in front of the cabin, a nice Bell Ranger helicopter.

Dakota shut down her Cessna as we watched two men coming out of our home. What the hell, I thought. It didn't take long for me to confront these two trespassers. I went at them fast. "What the hell do you think your doing, what gives you the right to come into my home?" They threw up their hand in front of them as if attempting to hold me back. " Mr McAuffe, were only doing our job." " What the hell job might that be and what the hell is this Mr McAuffe crap?" The oldest one about forty five or so spoke first. "We have orders to give you eviction notice, further more you have been observed illegally hunting on federal property." The veins in my neck must have stuck out a mile as I observed Dakota unsuccessfully moving to calm me down. I pushed the younger one aside and ran into the cabin. The next second found me with my dads old 30-06 pointing at them. "Now take it easy Mr McAuffe." "I'll take it easy, You have exactly ten seconds to get the hell off my strip." At that, they both started for me, the older one reached for his gun. I put a round at his feet. Just as fast, I loaded another shell and put that shot through the helicopters side window. They backed up and both got in. The younger one started the engine and in a cloud of dust they were gone.

I shook like a leaf as Dakota said, "Were in for it now Paul." "I know, what was I supposed to do? They had no right to come in here with that crap. We have never bothered any one. My family has lived here for over 50 years. I have all the right in the world to live here. No one has ever disputed that, or has any right to. My mother and father built this place and hunted the land as they needed all these years. Now some punk ass people from the government say I am trespassing and that I hunt illegally."

The peace of our home was shattered. All I wanted to do is write and live a quiet, contemplative life. Now I had to wait for them to return, as return they would. That was not long in coming. Two days later, two aircraft landed on our strip. It didn't take long for nine people to descended on us. I was not armed, and cuffs were quickly placed on my wrists. There was no time to say good by to Dakota while they whisked me away.

Anchorage was not the place I wanted to be, especially not in the city jail. They quickly booked me and placed me in with all sorts of people. People that I would never ordinally associate with. To go from total freedom to total loss of freedom is not my idea of the good life.

The arraignment was swift, if you want to call three days of bad food and bad company swift. Dakota had made arraignments for our family attorney to represent me. Keep in mind that the most he had ever had to do was a few wills and various papers. He had no experience in matters of the magnitude the government proposed. I had my doubts as to what he could do.

To listen to the prosecutor, you would have thought I was some big desperado. He talked about destruction of government property, unlawful poaching, attempted murder, resisting arrest and trespassing on government property. I am sure that if they could imagine anything else, that they would have thrown that in also.

Sam Littleton turned out to be much more formidable in the court room than I had imagined. He was unable to get me out on bail and I did have to wait three months for the trial but when he finally lit into his opponent, you would have thought the wrath of God turned loose.

In his closing argument he proved that the government had illegally entered my cabin. They had neglected to get a search warrant. They had no lawful orders of eviction, just their desire to get rid of residents with in the park boundary. They had not read me my rights, the list went on. Sam held the jury in the palm of his hand, telling them that I had enough Native American in me and the government had deprived me of my rights. He went on to say that my family had the right of existence on the land. His final clincher turned out to be some thing that I had not thought of.

Dad had always said that the cabin was on the Koyukuk River. I had never thought other wise. As it turned out we live on the Hammond River which flows into the Koyukuk. Not only that but after a costly survey, it was found that we live almost a mile south of the park boundary.

Not wanting to dwell on such an unpleasant affair, I will not go into all the details of the incarceration and trial. I do want to say that Sam did a hell of a good job for us.

The jury looked kindly on me and the judge had a field day with the government. I was free and able to return home. We found out later that the two rangers were reassigned. The oldest one is directing traffic at some park on the sea shore of Maine. The younger one now gives lectures to visitors in some grassland park. We did find out later that the two were very disappointed in their assignments. The judge did make me pay for the helicopter window and the repair of the exit hole in the opposite side of the chopper. He also said that he felt that I had the right to hunt the land as needed but suggested I consider getting a license.

Chapter 21

The Journal

Most of the summer for me was ruined. All that time in jail for no good reason left me more bitter toward authority than usual. As a family we have a long time feud ,with anyone who attempts to relieve us of our liberty. I recalled the stories told of long ago and how they dealt with the problem. My great grand dad John would have known how to handle things. I recalled his attitude toward the KKK when they came on his place. As a kid, I always thought it exciting when he leveled the old 10 gauge side hammer double barrel, on one hooded thug and pulled both triggers. I guess now days we are more civilized and have the law to protect us. The question still smoldered within me, where was the law when my privacy was shattered ? I could not get over the fact that it was the law that did the shattering.

Home at the cabin was not the same. It was nice to be back and it was nice to be with Dakota. I do love the place but I spent more and more time turning over recent events in my mind. The more I stewed over them, the worse it got. Dakota could not turn my interest toward other more pleasant things.

The days of fall got shorter and the nights colder. I continued to smolder with contempt. Dakota tried every thing she could to cheer me up. I spent days walking back and forth from the cabin to the end of the strip and back to the cabin. I wore a path in the strip as I paced back and forth. The time spent without freedom, where my every move was watched and permission had to be asked to pass gas, wore deep into my spirit. I knew that something had to give, when Dakota announced that she was leaving.

"I cant put up with your attitude any more Paul. I have tried every thing I know to turn you around. I have to get away for a while. I cant spend all my life with some one so bitter. Perhaps some time away will change both of us." The next morning found me on my knees crying as her bird flew out of site.

Breakfast later was a disaster. Every thing seemed to be a disaster. Even Tuk would not eat the burned food that I scrapped into his dish. How ungrateful I thought. I sat at the table toying with my cup of cold coffee, Tuk tried to snuggle up to me. Even that was of no help. I am ashamed to say that I pushed the poor little fellow away.

I did find my self thinking of something else besides the old problem as I thought how desperately I need to see my spirits, just talk with them for a while. The more I thought about that the more upset I got. Where in the hell were they when a person really needed them.

I stoked the fire in the old stove and prepared another breakfast. This time I took care to fix Tuk a special plate. How he loved bacon. As we finished our meal he looked up at me and my heart started to melt. We sat at the table for a long time. I stroked his fur and felt sorry that I treated him the way I did.

My eyes wandered around the cabin. The collection of a lifetime. The rifles and snowshoes on one wall along with old photos of the folks and the kids. Moms treasures were about the place along with dads. Marie was there as well as Dakota. The old tin box, the red blanket that Rachael gave Dakota, the list went on and on. My eyes passed over the book shelf and returned. I got up and walked over to it. I hadn't thought about the shelf in years. Dad, with his limited education was a big reader, especially after his conversion. His collection of the old classics, though not large revealed one book that I did not recall. I took it from the shelf, blew some dust off of the cover and sat down at the table.

The title touched me deeply. "Journal Of A Soul" by Pope John the 23rd. The book was thick and heavy as I scanned its many pages.

Time past quickly while I read this amazing story of one's journey through a life of faith. The many spiritual exercises left me wanting to read more. Day by day I came to realize that my soul also longed for more. I knew that I had always desired solitude over crowds and here was an inkling into a more profound spiritual path.

The stove gave off it's usual chugging sound as I contemplated one of the many thoughts that the book portrayed. Tuk lay curled up, one eye open, in the middle of the table next to the kerosene lamp. I lightly fingered the rim of my cup and was about to turn a page when I thought I heard a voice. No, I thought as I turned the page. "Paul."

There it was again. I looked around the room. All was quiet except the shallow breathing of Tuk and the sound of the stove. I continued reading for a couple more paragraphs only to hear it again. It was a mellow voice, nether male or female. A soft voice, soothing in the one word used. "Paul." There it was again. I once again looked around, this time getting up and opening the door. Nothing there except cold air, a night sky, and the far off sound of a lone wolf calling it's mate.

I thought of the voice from time to time over the next few days, certain that I had heard it but yet not so sure at the same time. Once again as I read in the evening, the same sounds of life and the same warm glow of the stove flowed through the room. This time in the middle of a paragraph, a thought came to me. I hadn't inhabited the events of the past summer a single time in days.

Time alone, time in deep contemplation of the story and the desire to change, brought change. In the next instant, the voice returned again. "What do you want?" I asked in anticipation of an answer. Silence—, I asked again, only to hear the same thing, nothing. This time I felt a slight stirring of the air in the room, Even Tuk popped his head up, but nothing else from him. "Paul, you are as stubborn as your father was all these years ago". This time I was sure that I heard a voice but then again it was more like some thing deep with in myself. Once again a slight movement of air within the room, this time from the direction of the stove. I looked at Tuk and he looked at me. We sat quietly for the longest time. Nothing else happened that evening.

I missed Dakota and my kids. By the calender, a month had passed since Dakota left. October, new fallen snow this morning, about four inches. Tuk and I went for a walk. It was funny watching Tuk up to his neck in four inches of snow. He made a valiant effort but soon begged for me to carry him. When we arrived at the end of the strip, I thought of Dakota and wished for her return. I thought about firing up the Cub and flying to Fairbanks but soon dismissed the idea. While we stood at the end of the strip it began to snow again. At first the flakes fell lazily, then bigger and faster.

Tuk and I returned to the cabin, I felt lucky that we found the cabin at all. As I looked over my shoulder, snow came down in a never ending cascade of white. I don't think that I had ever seen such an amount at one time.

I was glad that I had cleaned out the little hanger a few weeks before. The snow piled up so fast that it would have surely broken the Cubs wings had she been left outside.

Tuk and I were not exactly stranded, because I could pack down a strip with the snow machine. However there was no need to go anywhere. I no longer trap, or have any desire to do the things that once thrilled me in my youth. There is a certain advantage to having a snug cabin and plenty of food in the cache. Tuk was all the company I could stand at the time. The snow continued for several more days. It had to be a record of some kind. When it finally quit snowing it measured four and a half feet on the level.

Nothing to do but read and write, that is all I wanted in the first place. The snow blanketed the cabin roof and came half way up the cabin walls. It is good insulation. On occasion I had to open the door ajar because it became too warm.

Tuk occupied my lap as I continued to read. There it was again, the voice and the stirring of the air. I looked up to see a wisp of vapor in the corner in the simple form of a person. Nothing outstanding in features but I thought of Fr Paddy. It was an odd feeling, a little scarey and then again a little comforting. "Who are you?" No answer, and then it was gone and the cabin quiet as a tomb.

The thoughts of Fr Paddy continued occasionally through the evening hours. I thought of the times he visited my folks, the times he and my mother raced their dogs and the times that he and dad held long quiet conversations. As I read one particular passage, I recalled the Mass held in the cabin. I began to put all these things together. There is a link between the supernatural world of God and the seemingly detached pieces of our lives. God is with us in the every day world. It is just that we do not take the time to put two and two together. I vowed with the help of Gods grace to keep spiritual matters foremost in my mind.

Chapter 22

Bunny and Swift Antelope

Another two weeks past in contemplation of my life's worth. Days of grooming the strip with the snow machine and nights reading the Journal. Tuk and I became inseparable friends. Dakota returned on the fifth of November. The reunion sweet, in the arms of the person that mattered most in my life. Gone were any thoughts of the past summers trials.

Dakota left word with the kids when she left that I was not to be disturbed. She told them the state of my being and they reluctantly agreed to stay away. Dakota stayed around Fairbanks only long enough to pack a few things and get a ticket for South Dakota. The only family left alive lived on the Rosebud Reservation. All five brothers and sisters had returned there to live. They all shared some land out side of the little town of St Francis. Dakota said that life for them was not as good as it was when they lived on the home ranch in the Black Hills but they were around family on the reservation. Some were married and some were divorced. All made a living at what ever they could do.

The oldest brother told Lakota tales late into each night. That is when he was not drinking with his friends. None of the family had any faith. That is faith as seen by white men. Dakota said that all of them had a connection to the Great Spirit and regularly took part in medicine dances.

Dakota could not get over how all had changed in the few short years since she had seen them. She spent as much time with them as she could but wanted to return to her home on in the Brooks Range.

On the night before she left, her brother in a sober moment told her a story about a Great White Feather. The feather decided that it did not need the Great Eagle it came from, so left and floated a long way to earth. It floated so long and far that it ended up in Alaska. It found its home among other feathers like its self and in order to be happy needed to return to them. Dakota said that the tale made her realize that she had her family's blessing to leave and not worry about them any longer.

The older brother took her aside and asked her to take her sisters two children with her. He said that he realized that he had an alcohol problem and that her sister had one also. He felt it was in the best interest of the two kids to have a better chance at life with their Aunt Dakota.

Her sister was not opposed to the idea at all. In fact admitted that she could not provide for them and that they were having a lot of trouble at school. The kids were opposed to going so far away from their friends.

Perhaps I should explain the great surprise at seeing these two children as they got out of Dakota's bird. In my enthusiasm at seeing Dakota I did not think too much of it until Dakota announced her intentions.

Dakota fixed supper as I sat across the table from the two kids. They appeared sullen and non interested in their surroundings. Dakota had introduced them on their arrival but I had already forgotten the names. I got up and went for the coffee pot and started to reach for a little shot of rum for it as Dakota shook her head no.

Setting across from them once again, I asked their names. Both remained quiet. I asked again in a slightly raised voice. Finally the girl spoke. Meekly, she said her name was Bunny. The boy said nothing. I decided to ignore him for the time being and asked Bunny how old she was. Again very shyly and quietly she said "sixteen." "How old is your brother?" That got a response out of him. "I am fifteen, I am Lakota and I don't want to be here." Of course I had to reply, "Well you are here and you my fine friend are stuck, there is no way out unless you plan on a long walk." "I am Lakota and I can walk to the moon if I want," was his only reply. I couldn't resist as I said "Well you will freeze your ass off doing it."

Dakota fixed a fine meal and for once did not get on me for the condition of the skillet. After supper I went up to the loft and fixed up two beds for them. They sat around for a while as Dakota tried to interest them in their surroundings but they went to bed early with out so much as a thank you or good night.

Dakota and I had a lengthy discussion in hushed tones, for the better part of two hours. I had hoped for peace and quiet in my old age and Dakota was talking of adoption.

Sleep did not come for quite a while. I did manage to talk to my Lord about the situation but heard no answers. How in the world was I going to adjust to two sullen strangers in my life? The only thing I thought I heard as I drifted off was "I was a stranger and you took me in."

I danced out of bed and across the cold floor. Stoking the fire I put the coffee pot on to boil. Out the door for morning chores and back in as fast as possible. I took another look at the fire and loaded more wood in. As was my usual habit, I watched the grounds swirl in the pot. About the time I was about to poor a cup, the boy spoke. 'It's hot up here." I suppose that I was playing his game when I said, "Not as hot as its going to be if you don't get down here." He came down the ladder only to find the temperature of the bed to be more inviting. Up the ladder he went but shortly nature won out and he was back down the ladder. "Where's the bathroom?" I went over to the window and scraped the frost off. Peeking out side, I said "Its 36 below, if you hurry you can make a run for it and be back before you freeze to death"."

He didn't take as long as I thought. The boy stood around the stove shivering like a leaf. " I thought you said that you are Lakota and can do anything." That did not get much of a response. I put the skillet on the fire and proceeded to lay in about half a pound of bacon. "You hungry?" Now I was getting to him. "Yes, but I've never seen so much bacon in my life." "Well get used to it, You will need all the food you can eat, to keep away the cold. Now that I know that you can talk, I'll ask again, Lakota, what's you name?" The response was short and to the point. "Jacob".

"Well Jacob, that's a good name, my grandfathers name was Jacob. They called him Jake, or Jack Ass for short. My other grand fathers name was Charlie Two Bears." Jacob said that he preferred Charlie Two Bears, said that it was a good Indian name. "Ah, but it wasn't an Indian name in his case, he was an Eskimo." Jacob had to think about

that one. He said that one of his grand fathers was Swift Antelope."
"Well that's a good name, how would you like it if I called you Swift
Antelope?"

The boy beamed from ear to ear. "You mean it, can I really use
my grand fathers name?" I had to think fast, and said "you can if I
say you can. Look, as fast as you went out side and back a little while
ago, I figure you must be as fast as a Swift Antelope."

Swift Antelope peered into the skillet as I turned the bacon.
Bunny came down the ladder at the same time that Dakota got up.
Both were out the door and back in no time. Swift Antelope asked me
if he could cook the eggs. I said sure, as he looked around for them.
"Where they at?" "Right here in the box, there powdered. Here let
me show you how its done."

The girls sat at the table as we served breakfast. Bunny had to say
some thing just as I was about to think that the ice was broken. "I'm
not going to eat that, if he cooked it." I lied and said that I cooked it
and that ended the first skirmish.

We sat down with the girls, I introduced Swift Antelope. Dakota
looked at me as I winked. "Swift Antelope, now that's nice and how
did we come to that name?" "It's a long story hon, I'll explain later."
That was not the end of it though as Bunny said Swift Antelope and
turned up her nose. I looked across the table at her for a long minute.
"Bunny, if I say it's Swift Antelope, than it's Swift Antelope. Perhaps
if he has the name of one of his grand fathers, he will act like it and
do his grand father proud, end of conversation."

I thought it a good opportunity to introduce Swift Antelope to
bringing in the wood. Dakota had other ideas. "OK kids it's time for
school." That lit every ones fire for sure. Both of them rebelled. "What
do we need school for? how far is it? we don't need education." There
was more but the list is too long to go into.

Dakota got up, went to a big box and pulled out it's contents.
"I took the liberty to go to the school in Fairbanks and get their
recommendation for home schooling. I then bought everything that
you two will need to finish school. There will be no discussion on the
subject. I will teach you, and you will learn. There will be classes five
days a week, six days, until you get caught up. The faster you learn
the sooner you graduate. It's up to you. By the way, you will also learn

the Lakota language." I had to admit she was right and admired her for her stand.

I popped in and out of the cabin all morning as I did some work in the hanger. Dakota had things well in hand. At lunch I looked over some of the books that they were using. Basic math, history, english, as well as several other books. Both were at the seventh or eighth grade level. I asked Dakota about it and she said that she felt that both were behind where they should be for their age.

I took over the cooking chores, to give Dakota more time with the classes. As I prepared supper and classes over, Bunny came over to watch me. I had a nice moose roast about ready to go into the oven. "What's that?" "Well girl, its moose." Knowing she most likely had never had it, I asked if she liked it. "How should I know?" I asked what she meant. "I've never even heard of moose. What is it?" I couldn't believe that a sixteen year old didn't know what a moose was. "You know what a buffalo looks like?" "Yes, but I've never seen one except on television." She followed with a question while I still tried to process a Native American never seeing a buffalo.

Swift Antelope piped in, "I've seen lots of buffalo." Bunny remarked, "You have not, only on television. Where is your television? I'm missing my soaps." Swift Antelope said, "I'm not finished, I saw lots of them when my uncle took me to Custer Park." Bunny had to come back with, "You have never been to Custer Park." "Have to." "Have not." "Have to, last summer when he went to Edgemont and Rapid City. He asked me if I wanted to go. Said he wanted me to go in this place and pick up a package for him. So there."

"We don't have television Bunny, in case you haven't noticed we don't have power." "What do we do besides take dumb old classes, everybody has TV." I suddenly I felt like I lived in the 18th century, no television. "Well girl we have never needed such a thing up here, there are too many other things to do besides watch TV." Getting in the last word she replied "Like what, set around and watch each other breathe?" I let it go and I must say the two kids dove into the moose. I never heard anyone say that they didn't like it. After supper the kids were put to work with the dishes. A few squabbles arose but Dakota put them down quickly.

While the kids did some assigned reading before bed, Dakota and I conversed about their future. Once they were asleep Dakota told me she wanted to tell me something. I couldn't imagine what it was but listened as she held my hand across the table. "Paul, there is something I have to tell you. I have been waiting for the right time with the excitement of the kids and all. When I got back to Fairbanks I learned of the death of our good friend. There is no way to put it delicately. Father Paddy died in his sleep last month. Before you get upset, remember that I told the kids not to disturb you under any circumstances. I take the blame for you not knowing."

I caught my breath and told Dakota what I had experienced while I read from the journal. "I think that he came to visit me one last time, in fact I'm sure of it. I could feel him here with me. I will miss the old gent. One of the last, Sled Dog Priests." We talked of the occurrence and my new found freedom . Dakota told me that God does not close one door with out opening another one. "You know Paul, these kids need us as much as we need them. Perhaps it's meant to be this way. You are a good man Paul and you have much to teach them. You would not believe the things these two have had to endure. They are behind because of the system and the circumstances they lived under. No one seemed to care for them and how they turned out. Their own mother did not want them. There was hardly a time while I was there that she and most of the others weren't drunk or high on something. I am glad that my brother had a sober moment and asked me to take them."

I squeezed her hand and winked, "I'm glad you brought them woman. I fell in love with these two the moment I realized they were here. I know it's not going to be easy but we can do it." It was bed time. I slept sound for the first time in quite a while, knowing that I had a new family. If my peace and quiet was shattered, so be it. God grant me wisdom.

Chapter 23

Lessons of Life

Bunny and Swift Antelope rebelled the first two days but slowly got into the rhythm of study as Dakota led them into new ground. I loved watching and listening to her as they journeyed through the lessons. I really enjoyed it as she started their adventure into the Lakota language. Dakota told me that she was very rusty and that she had to think long and hard to recall the language she learned from her mother.

I labored all week to get the snow machine in good working order. Their first Saturday with us broke with the temperature at only ten below. After breakfast I took Swift Antelope out to the hanger and threw the tarp off of the old machine. He just stood there as if he had no idea as to what it was. "Ever seen one of these things?" He admitted he had, once. He never knew what it was for.

After a few tries she fired up in a cloud of blue smoke as I watched his eyes widen. "Hop on" and at that, we were off. I poured the coals to her as she planed on the now crusted snow. At the end of the strip I did a wide turn but he was not ready and flew through the air for fifteen or twenty feet. I went back as he extracted him self from the snow. Swift Antelope laughed his butt off and was hooked.

When we returned to the cabin, I jumped off and told him to hit it. Off he went as the tracks dug in. Keep in mind that this was an ancient machine and I did not consider it to be very fast. He must have thought that he was doing ninety as he rounded the end of the strip with her wide open. Bunny and Dakota came out the door to see what all the commotion was about.

I managed to get him off of it while telling Bunny to get on. Reluctant at first, it took only one round of the strip and the rest of the day was taken up with arguments as to who's turn it was next.

Sunday was much the same as they put mile after mile on the old relic. Dakota and I would occasionally go to the window to watch the show. It was good to see them doing something that I knew they would enjoy. Dakota remarked, "you know Paul that you have started something." "I guess I have."

Thanksgiving came in with a bang. Joe, his wife, the twins, and Dave, all got out of the first plane. Not ten minutes later Ladonna and Al as well as Ian and Peggy got out of the second one.

I had a plan and had to act quickly. I did not know that Ian was coming at all. I had been planning for months, to get him the next time I saw him. I quickly enlisted Swift Antelope in my scheme. We filled about five pounds of flour into a paper bag. We tied a string to it and I boosted Swift Antelope up into the rafters to hold the bag. On my signal he was to let the bag swing into the open door. I thought my plan and timing perfect. At the last minute Ian opened the door and was about to enter the cabin. I signaled Swift Antelope to let her go. At the last second Ian stopped and bowed to Peggy and bid her enter first. The rest is history.

Dakota had to let me know that enlisting Swift Antelope into my plan was not the brightest idea I ever had. We spent an hour getting Peggy cleaned up and I got a crushing hand shake and slap on the back anyway. Ian thought it the greatest joke in the world. I don't think he ever caught on that the joke was for him. Of course this did not endear me to Peggy who I had been trying to impress since we first met.

I hadn't considered the fact that my kids had already met Bunny and Swift Antelope. Ladonna and Bunny got along as though they had known each other all their lives. Ladonna did comment later that she could not get over the change in the two. I was asked by all three about Swift Antelopes name. I just told them I would tell them some time and left it at that.

Once Peggy looked a little more presentable she took over the kitchen. I noticed Bunny watching her every move. Then to my surprise she asked Peggy if she could help. Peggy took to her right away and started teaching the tricks of a five star chef.

The table set, all sat down where ever they could find a spot. We started to dig in when Dakota put a halt to us. "Paul, I believe that you have an obligation?" "Oh yes, I almost forgot." I didn't almost forget, I was so interested in Peggy's cooking that I couldn't wait.

" Father, we thank you for this very fine looking meal. We thank you for all here present. We ask you to remember the sick, the hungry, and the homeless. We also want to welcome our new children into our family, lets eat, amen."

When I complemented Peggy on the fine meal she looked at me as though I had committed some great sin or something. She did say however that she would not have been able to do it, if it wasn't for Bunny. To this, Bunny beamed from ear to ear.

We had a couple of drinks after dinner in remembrance of Fr. Paddy but nothing like the usual. Dakota would not stand for it. She had told me prior, that she did not want the children to have to be associated with it any longer. There was no argument from me on that part. Since I met Dakota I had been drinking less and less and felt better for it. Of course a wee dram of rum in my coffee from time to time suited me just fine.

I took Joe aside after dinner and told him of my idea for Christmas for the kids. He readily agreed in his slow methodical speech and I knew it was all set. Ian and Peggy announced their plans for a lodge. They were on this trip to find a place that could be serviced by our aircraft. They said that they had looked far and wide but found nothing that was wild and remote enough but yet was with in flying range. He said that the locations that he wanted were taken up by the government. I had to agree and as he did not know as yet of my brush with the law, I told the story.

We agreed to sit down with the map the next day and find a great spot. The hour became late and all settled in for the night. As I shut my eyes I thought of gratitude for our many blessings.

All too soon they were gone. How the twins had grown. I was so pleased the way Bunny pitched in with them. All the kids were doing well, that is except for Joe. I worried about him and asked once again for his healing. His speech became more slurred every time I saw him. His mind still seemed to be sharp and I was sure he would carry out my Christmas surprise.

As Christmas approached Bunny and Swift Antelope seemed disinterested. I asked Dakota what she thought the reason to be. I got an ear full. They had never had a Christmas. At least not one filled with the joy of giving and receiving gifts. I hadn't told Dakota of my plan and she never hinted at hers.

Christmas eve had a clear cold sky. I walked the kids out to the end of the strip for their first real view of the Northern Lights. They were in awe as the lights seemed to put on a special show just for them. We stayed out for a long time. Long enough for Dakota to start her plan.

Eyes were as big as saucers as we entered to the darkened cabin. The little Christmas tree sparkled in the light of the candles. Little shadows played on the walls of the cabin. Dakota laid out her special desert and we all dug in. You could tell that this was a special treat for the kids and they let us know with the first hugs that we had received from them.

Early on Christmas morning I could hear the large twin rotor helicopter as it approached. I was dressed and ready. Slung from beneath on palettes were four brand new snow machines, ready to go. We had them off loaded before any one even woke. The chopper departed in a storm of swirling snow as the pilot gave a hardy wave. I even thought I heard a Ho! Ho! Ho! as the crew chief kicked out a very large bundle.

Surly every one would wake but they didn't. That chopper made enough noise to wake the dead. I took the opportunity to throw a tarp over the machines and drag in the big package. Still no one woke. There were stirring's though as I quietly opened the big bundle and laid out the packages. With every thing in order, I stoked the fire and sat down with a cup. Tuk licked my hand.

Dakota dressed and I handed her a cup. As she sat, I gave her a long hug and wished her a Merry Christmas. We sat and talked for the better part of an hour before we heard rustling from the loft. Bunny rubbing sleep from her eyes was first down the ladder, followed by Swift Antelope. I sat in total anticipation of their seeing all the gifts spread out all over the floor. I think Dakota had the same feelings as I did as she gave me that look of hers. How could these teenagers possibly not see what lay in store for them?

"Merry Christmas kids!" Sterile looks, were returned. Dakota asked what was up with them. "Nothing," they both replied. "Aren't you excited to see all these gifts? There for you."

Bunnies answer floored me. "We've never had gifts for Christmas! We didn't know that they were for us." I had to speak out, "What do you mean no gifts? I cant imagine Christmas with out gifts." I got up, threw my parka on and in frustration, went outside. As I stood on the porch looking at the tarp covered snow machines my mind raced for an answer. How could any one not know about gifts at Christmas?

Dakota opened the door and told me to get inside. There on the floor were both of them ripping and tearing wrappers one after another. The light in their eyes bright and smiles abounding. I asked Dakota what happened. "Well Paul, they truly do not know the meaning of Christmas. I am appalled that my family never gave them any thing. Never taught them the meaning of Christmas. I shouldn't be surprised though, the way they drink up all their money."

Bunny held up a new fur parka from Ladonna and a hand full of cookbooks from Peggy. Swift Antelope ripped into a long box to find a brand new 308 rifle from Dave. Next came a new hunting knife from Al, as well as ammunition from Joe. Both happened to open gifts from Ian at the same time. Beautiful Mukluks, I asked the kids where they were made and what they were made of. Of course they had no answers as they put them on. "Well guys, Ian most likely picked them up on his travels to Baffin Island. They are hand made as you can see. They will keep you warm out on the trail." Next Swift Antelope picked up a large box, ripped it open and pulled out another beautiful red nylon shell parka with a wolverine ruff, from Dakota. I asked Swift Antelope if he knew what the fur was and he had to say no. "The fur is wolverine, the reason that it is used is because it will not frost up as much as other furs." Bunny pulled seal skin and moose hide mittens from a bag. Next from the bag came girl stuff. Perfume, lipstick and I don't know what all. I said " what you need all that girl stuff for?" She just blushed as Dakota gave me a kick from under the table. Swift Antelope opened a box from Joe's wife. In it he found mittens made of wolf and beaver.

Dakota handed me a small package. It had a wrapping of gold paper with a red ribbon. "Here Paul, I picked this up in Rapid City for you before I went out to the reservation. The box contained one fantastically beautiful Black Hills Gold pocket watch. As I opened the cover I saw a picture of Dakota. Tears came to my eyes as she said to read the inscription on the back. TO MY BELOVED HUSBAND AND FRIEND, DAKOTA.

"We didn't get you any thing" Bunny said. Swift Antelope made the same remark. " Well kids, you have given us more than you can imagine. You have opened up a whole new life for us."

Dakota looked a little hurt as she got nothing from me. I caught that look and said wait a few minutes and you will see. "OK kids lets eat and by the way, no one is permitted out side till I say so."

We had a light breakfast and it was on with the new parkas, mittens, and mukluks. I think they must have caught on to something as they all went out the door faster than usual. Once outside the hanger, I ripped the tarp from the machines.

The jumping up and down and cheers were worth it. Dakota jumping the most. I tried to quickly go through basic safety and maintenance instructions but the first engine was started by Dakota before I could finish. Then Swift Antelope followed by Bunny. Before I could think to jump on and start mine, they were at it, full bore down the strip. Before I could catch up, they were back at the cabin. They made a quick left and hit one of moms old trails. Dakota in the lead, followed by Swift Antelope who had passed Bunny on the cabin turn. The machines threw a roster tail of snow from the tracks ten feet in the air as I struggled to catch up. As I rounded a turn in the trail I should have seen them. They were out of site.

We spent the day riding trails that I hadn't seen in years. I finally caught up with them about noon. We cut a trail half way across the river and made another left. About two in the afternoon and about out of fuel we arrived back at the cabin. Tuk was very glad to see us.

With all the excitement, I plumb forgot to tell Tuk's part of the story. We cant leave Tuk out. He loves the kids and has taken to sleeping with Bunny. The first night she was here, he sat at the ladder begging her to lift him up. He follows her every where in the cabin that she might be. He is gaining weight as Bunny constantly feeds him from her plate.

Oh yes, he got a new sweater for Christmas.

Swift Antelope thinks the dog is too small for him. Says he had a big dog once. Said his uncle shot him for no good reason. I did not press the issue and let it pass.

Bunny and I fixed lunch and then Swift Antelope and I had a shooting contest. I felt sorry for this fifteen year old who had never shot a rifle. After some basic instruction, he took to it right away. We sat some cans up at the end of the strip and shot for about an hour. I have to admit that he was the better shot. We'll have to do some hunting soon.

The rest of the day passed quietly with Bunny pouring over her new books and Swift Antelope cleaning his rifle and admiring his shiny new knife. Dakota announced that school waited in the morning. The kids tried to rebel but gave up as Dakota announced that there would be no snow machines, if school work was not done.

We found it hard to believe the change in Bunny and Swift Antelope. They had their moments but generally were no longer sullen and defiant. Life with them turned out to be a blessing. We really did have a new life and a new family.

They were catching up fast with Dakota's firm hand and grasp of their needs. They still had class six days a week but with shorter hours. Bunny loved to cook and started experimenting by changing recipes she had mastered in the cook books. I soon was relegated to second cook. Swift Antelope and I more or less did the dishes and gave Dakota a break. Each lesson for the kids, required much of her time in preparation.

One day Dakota, as I sat in my usual posture at the table, enjoying my third cup of coffee, announced a new teacher. I thought I heard something about a new history professor. Being slow of wit on occasion, I did not realize who the new teacher was to be, until I heard my name mentioned.

I have to admit a certain turmoil that night as I tossed and turned trying to figure out what to do. When I asked Dakota about it the next morning, she just said to be my self. After morning chores, I sat down with their history book. I read and the more I read, the more I thought about who my students were. This stuff would have to be taught at some point but not to these two and not now.

I had some nervousness as I took over for the next morning. Dakota smiled her sweet smile as I started. "Do you know the date of the founding of our country? Do you know about the Louisiana purchase? Do you know about Lewis and Clark or Washington?" Blank stares.

"Well I'm putting you on. I don't know much about that stuff either. Eventually we will have to learn it, in order for you to graduate. We are not going to do that now. For now we will learn about Crazy Horse, Sitting Bull, Chief Joseph and any thing else having to do with the history of the Native American Peoples. We will also tell stories, stories about our own people. This is as much history as any school book. I hope you will find it interesting enough to come to enjoy it as much as I do."

They sat in rapt attention as I told them of Paul, Rachael and Simon. I told them of their travels on the Ohio River in the sixteen hundreds, The close calls with hostels and their bowmanship. We talked of exploration and ship wreck, of the Scottish people of our family. We related family history to national history.

By the end of the first day I was exhausted. They had their assignment. Find one story about their people that they could tell, then write about it.

The next morning I announced our history lesson for the day. We are going to take the snow machines and learn about the history of hunting. At that Dakota thought I was stretching the issue a little. After I told her of my plan she relented.

Dakota stayed behind with Tuk as Bunny, Swift Antelope and I, dressed in our finest cold weather gear and took off. Dakota packed a fine lunch with coffee and cocoa in our thermoses. We carried extra fuel on the back of one machine and each of us had a rifle slung over our shoulders. Bunny had no experience at all with hunting and Swift Antelope only with target practice under his belt.

As far as I was concerned, this would be fun. I recalled the words of the judge when he suggested I get a license. What did I need a license for, hell I was teaching two Indians what they should have known for years.

I knew a place about twenty miles South West of the cabin, always good for a moose. We moved slowly as I broke trail. About an hour out from the cabin I stopped at the edge of a small frozen pond. The air lay still as vapor hit the cold air from a hole in the ice. The snow lay thick over the frozen water with a hump smack in the middle.

We sat on the machines with a warm drink cradled in our hands as I asked the kids what they supposed the hump to be. Bunny thought it an old Igloo. I asked her why. "I saw a picture of one in a magazine once." I asked Swift Antelope what he thought. "I don't know. Is it a sleeping bear?"

"It's a beaver house. I know it sort of looks like an Igloo Bunny but there are no Igloos in Alaska." I went on, " Bears don't hibernate in the open like that, besides it's too big to be a bear, Swift Antelope." They both asked "what is it?"

"Looks like a beaver house to me. See the hole in the ice? Look closer and you will see little tracks coming up out of the water. They go almost in a straight line to those willows." I went on, They must be a little short of food. I think they don't like leaving their warm house too much in the winter. See the way those willows are chewed off?"

The kids put the lids on their thermoses and went over to the trees. In a minute they called to me to come and see. Bunny said " look there are more tracks." I asked them what they meant. " Swift Antelope excitedly said, "wolf". Bunny thought it a small dog. "Well both of you are close but not correct." They exclaimed, "Well what is it?"

"Fox, you see the other tracks? They are ptarmigan. Look over there, see the white bird just pecking at the willow branch?" Both of the kids looked as intently as they could. Finally I pointed and quietly said, "there, see, next to that stump the beaver left." Suddenly both the kids saw the bird. "Wow what a pretty bird" Bunny said. I had to mention that the ptarmigan are more a grey brown in the summer and turn white in the winter. The realization of a winter world opened up before the kids, as they found more tracks. "Looks like a jack rabbit" came first from Swift Antelope. "Nope, varying hare, some call it a snow shoe rabbit though." All of a sudden they were seeing tracks all over the place. I asked, "What has been going on here?" I started getting explanations that made sense. The kids were opening themselves up to a wider world.

My lesson for the day. "You have to know what is in your world before you can live successfully in it. In this case it is the Arctic. In the case of some one who lives, say, in a city, it is something else. They have to know one thing and you another. Our people have been hunting and living off the land for centuries. The Lakota had to know the animals of the land as much as you have to know the animals of the Arctic. They hunted antelope, buffalo and wild birds to name a few. You will hunt bears, moose, caribou, wolves and a whole host of Arctic animals. That's the lesson for the day, lets hunt."

As we moved closer to what I always called my sure thing spot, we got off the machines and waded through hip deep snow, for about one hundred yards. Bunny was the first to spot him. A nice young bull, small antlers, too busy chomping on some willow bark to notice us. I motioned for quiet. We had all the time in the world. I quietly showed Bunny how to chamber a round and operate the safety, and look through the site. Swift Antelope already had it accomplished. The moose on hearing the second round being chambered raised his head. "Now both of you, don't get buck fever." Both the kids shook with excitement. Both rifles went off at the same time. The moose dropped in his tracks.

You talk about two excited hunters. They certainly got to the moose much faster than I did. When I finally got there I asked where they hit him. One hit was evident, straight through the chest. It wasn't until we got him gutted, cut, and quartered that we found the second hole. Straight through the rump. "Now which one of you killed him?" Both claimed the kill. The argument was on, 'I did.' "No I did." I knew this discussion would go on all their adult lives. When ever hunting stories would come up, what ever camp fire they sat around, it would remain till the day they died.

Chapter 24

The Gift of Books

What little day light available to us, left an hour before we finished packing the moose on the machines. The trip home was easier because the trail was already broken. Running a trail at night has it's own rewards. The snow glistens in the light of the head lights. Shadows play across the landscape in ever changing variations.

Before we could go into the cabin we had to hang the meat high in the hanger to keep the critters from stealing it. Dakota and Tuk awaited our arrival with anticipation. We shucked our parkas and other clothing in a pile on the floor, much to Dakota's dislike. Supper though slightly over done setting in the oven, proved to be fit for a king. Bunny and Swift Antelope held Dakota's attention with the most amazing tale of the hunt. If I were embellishing it for the sport of a gang of cronies, I could not have done better. That episode led me to believe that we had some very good story tellers on our hands.

When they finally calmed down I said, "I hate to burst your bubble but we have meat to cut up. We spent the rest of the evening and well past midnight preparing the moose for the cache. We had two worn out kids on our hands by the time we finished.

To my surprise they were up and at it early the next morning. Bunny had the skillet going with fresh moose steaks, eggs, and potatoes from the root cellar. Swift Antelope came through the door with an arm load of wood and just missed Tuk as he dumped it into the wood box. I was so tired that I could hardly move. I suppose I was a bit older and didn't want to admit it. We ate leisurely and Dakota took pity on the kids and didn't start class until the afternoon.

By the time breakfast was over, I had been fully informed of Dakota's plan. We had discussed adoption without the kids knowing about it. The weather the last few days had been suitable for flying and Dakota wanted to go to town. When informed of the trip the kids jumped at the chance. I for one missed them before they left. Swift Antelope, Bunny and I pre flighted Dakota's plane. I relished the opportunity to teach them something that I knew well. They didn't disappoint me. They had more questions than I was ready to answer. Secretly I smiled at the thought of two more pilots in the family.

They were off, before the short day light penetrated the winter sky. In a too familiar roar they were gone. Alone, I stood there without moving until I could no longer hear them. I silently prayed for their safety.

Dakota planned to be gone for two weeks. Two weeks, I thought. How will I ever survive two weeks without my new family? I kicked the snow a bit and headed for the cabin. Two weeks I thought, two whole weeks.

I re stoked the fire and put the pot on to boil. Tuk, ever present in the folds of my parka was glad to be let out. "Well boy what are we going to do for two whole weeks?" Of course he had no answer. He laid on the table in his usual spot. Everyone had long ago given up trying to keep him down. The cup steamed in my hand as I turned the pages of the journal. I read and reread chapters of the Pope's writings. I couldn't get over how it affected me. After all, they were just narratives of retreats that he had taken over his lifetime. Shouldn't be much concern to me but it was.

Out of the blue, without warning or forethought, I began to pray. Of course for my family but even deeper. For those that I had offended in the past. For those I had forgotten. For all that I may meet in the future. Thanksgiving abounded. For all that I had. For those that were in my care. For every one who crossed my path. The list went on and on. Strangely, a hush fell over the room. A hush even more so than ever before. There it was again the presence with in the room as well as my self. Stirring's of form with out matter. Here there and through out the room. A feeling of peace, of well being. The voice began at a low pitch, growing ever so slightly, until I could almost hear it. "Paul, Paul." Then silence. The presence remained as I attempted to ignore it. Not that a person can ignore such a thing. Could I have been playing a game with the presence? Then as quickly as it came, the mood returned to the winter chug of the stove.

Tuk and I ate heartedly. We split a moose steak, black on the outside and almost rare in the middle. It's always amazing, the amount that the little dog can eat or the great belch he is capable of. I poured another cup and happened to glance into the skillet. I should have cleaned it but thought, another time.

About three hours after supper, the voice returned. Again faint at first, then a little louder. "Paul." This time I said "yes, go ahead I can hear you." Once again the silence was repeated. I waited for about fifteen minutes then repeated, "I'm right here, what do you want?" The peace returned, the presence returned, then, "I want you." I asked, "What do you mean, I want you?"

The next morning as Tuk and I finished breakfast, I pondered the meaning of the voice. I couldn't imagine what it meant or why. I slipped Tuk inside my parka as we slipped out the door to do something, I don't recall what. I do recall looking up and seeing the two dogs, Spirit and Broken Eye down at the end of the strip. I called to them but they just sat. I began to walk toward them but they disappeared.

As I sat at the table, Tuk worked his little jaws around a large bone. His little growl menaced some unseen intruder. In an instant the two dogs appeared. Spirit grabbed the bone as Tuk charged. Broken Eye ran interference as Tuk plucked the bone from the great jaws of Spirit. At first I thought that trouble brewed but soon realized that a great game unfolded. I proceeded to get into it my self as all four of us landed in a pile in the middle of the big bear skin rug. I was happy to see my old friends to say the least.

I scraped a few blackened particles aside in the skillet and fixed another supper. The dogs never tired of my cooking. The evening progressed with the temperature plunging to minus thirty five. The usual chug of the stove broken only by the snores of the dogs. All three laid out on the rug with Tuk in the middle. Once again I prayed as I read. Then the voice returned. This time there was no mistaking it. It was loud and clear. "Paul, Paul, I want you." I had about reached the limit of my patience and replied "I want you, to what?" "Paul, I want you to clean the skillet."

The two weeks, turned out to be only a week and a half. While Tuk and I did chores out side, I heard the unmistakable sound of

Dakota's engine. She made a wide bank and came in slow, almost like a gull landing on water.

As my family got out, I had three happy people to greet me. Swift Antelope and I pulled the plane into the hanger as Dakota and Bunny carried packages into the cabin.

Supper was a joyous affair. Dakota couldn't get over the fact that the skillet gleamed. "Paul, I've never seen the skillet look so good." I had to tell her the story. She just laughed and explained that she had thought of me and the old skillet and hoped that I didn't get food poisoning.

I wondered where the dogs went while Bunny, brimming over with excitement told of her landing. That broke my thoughts, "Your landing?" "Yes, you should have seen it, it was so cool." "Bunny, I did see it, you did that?" "I did it with Aunt Dakota's help." I looked at Dakota, trying to hide my thrill and be stern at the same time. Dakota shrugged and replied "I do believe that you soloed at thirteen."

I told Bunny that I was proud of her and how the landing looked from the ground. You could see the pride build in her. Of course Swift Antelope had to put in his two cents. " I could have done better. When can I fly? She's a girl, girls aren't supposed to fly."

Now I have known Dakota long enough to realize that one never tells her that girls aren't supposed to fly. Before she could get a word in, I asked him who he thought his Aunt was. "She's a girl isn't she?" He had to admit that she was but begrudgingly. Any way that seemed to defuse the potential situation. My final word on the subject, told him that I would have to see more improvement in his school work before he flew.

The packages contained nothing but necessary items, such as clothing and more girl stuff. Dakota told Bunny to put the items away as we sat down. I asked her about the adoption. "I went to our lawyer and told him what we wanted. He took all the information and had me call the next day. I suppose he thought that contacting some one on the Rosebud Reservation was like calling down the street. Any way when I went back to see him he told me that there was no reply. I took the liberty to have him get a lawyer in Rapid City to get the papers started. You know Paul, this is not going to be easy. I hope after all the trouble, that she won't change her mind."

I hadn't thought about that and began to worry. I could not imagine, not adopting these two great kids. I had grown more attached to them every day and told Dakota so.

"Oh!" Dakota jumped up, "I almost forgot, Swift Antelope, will you go out to my plane and get the large box in the back? Dear will you help him?" Swift Antelope started out the door without his parka as boys will do. "Put your parka on, its cold out there." "Aunt Dakota, it's only thirty six below", as he scraped the frost and looked at the thermometer.

How could Dakota forget such a large box? We struggled to get the box out of the plane and onto one of the sleds. Both of us tugged and pulled the box up to the cabin door. I hollered for Dakota to open the door as we hurriedly went in and put the box on the table. "Whew, what in tarnation you got in that thing?" "I have no idea Paul, lets have a guessing game." We all thought that Dakota had a good idea, as one after another tried to guess the contents. Swift Antelope thought it a box full of rocks. Bunny, having not lifted it as yet, gave the corner a small nudge. The box of course didn't move. The next time she gave a mighty heave and almost tipped it over. Each of us missed the guess as Swift Antelope took his big hunting knife and slit open the top. The first thing we saw was a note.

Dear kids, we hope that with these books, you will learn to appreciate your heritage. Happy reading. Al and Ladonna.

Dakota responded with "what a nice thought, remember kids to thank them when we see them." We each dove into the box, picking the books up and exclaiming the titles.

One book on Crazy Horse, one book on Chief Joseph, and three books on the Battle of Wounded Knee. There were books on Native American affairs as well as several books on the Army's part in the so called taming of the west. Books on General Crook, General Sheridan as well as several other generals that I had never heard of. Bunny picked over the titles that she had more interest in. Basket weaving as done by North West Peoples and several that told of cooking in the Native fashion.

Swift Antelope found several of interest. One being a rather thick book narrating the Trail of Tears. One seemed to hold particular interest. It happened to be tales about Lakota People.

I found several that told of the Hopi and Navajo. All in all there must have been close to seventy five books. Dakota informed me that as family historian, it was up to me to read them all. "How else are you going to teach history unless you know the subject?" I silently groaned at the thought of all that reading but actually looked forward to getting into it.

The silence of a winter afternoon was broken occasionally by the sounds of turning pages and an occasional change of position by one or all. Once as I looked up to rest my eyes, the thought of the two kids deep into reading charged my soul. It had really only been weeks since their arrival and yet they had made so much progress. The change in them from the first day amazed me.

Tuk broke the peace as he suddenly jumped from my lap and went for his food dish. Finding it empty, one paw deftly placed, flipped it over with a clank. Looking at me, I thought I heard him say "what's this?" Of course we know that dogs can't talk, or can they? At that, Dakota got up to fix supper. Bunny, right behind her suggested that she be allowed to try a new recipe that she had just read about.

Supper was great. I cant tell you what the recipe entailed but the sweet aroma of the moose roast made my mouth water as the oven door was opened several times.

Chapter 25

Rejection

The winter progressed, broken by hunting on snow machines, long afternoons of quiet reading and school. Then as fate would have it, our family life became complicated. Dave dropped in early one morning with two passengers and a load of supplies.

Our lawyer Sam, disembarked first and helped an obviously inebriated, frail looking woman from the door. Or should I say tried desperately to keep his balance as she collapsed in a heap, in the new fallen snow.

I rushed to help her but noticed Swift Antelope held back. As she sat up, she spoke with a slur, "come help your mother up, you son of a bitch." Swift Antelope just turned and went to the cabin.

"Paul, meet your sister in-law, Sparkling Water. Let's get her into the cabin before she freezes." " There's little chance of that." I said as I also thought, she's got too much anti freeze in her to freeze. I also thought that she was aptly named. It took both of us to drag her to the cabin. Once inside I told Swift Antelope to help Dave unload the plane. As we laid her down on the bed Dakota covered her, then went to the stove to make a strong pot of coffee. Bunny did not greet her mother and went to help Dave.

She slept it off as Dakota, Sam and I sat at the table now and then glancing in her direction. Dakota was in tears. Sam said that her brother had sent him a message, saying that she was on her way, to see her kids and that he should be ready for anything. "Anything was right. They had to drag her off the plane in Fairbanks and were none too glad to put her in my care." Sam went on to say that he got hold of Joe and his wife and together they put her into Dave's plane and the rest was history.

Bunny once again cooked supper and we all ate silently as various grunts and snores came from the bed. Suddenly as I was about to take a big bite of Bunny's fine food, B-A-R-F, the biggest, longest barf I ever heard. Dakota, ever the nurse, went to her sister in a flash as I tried to hold down my supper. The kids just looked at each other and shook their heads.

I took the kids for a long walk to the end of the strip. There, I can usually find the peace that I need in times of trouble. This time I laid it out to the kids. I told them of Dakota and my plans and hopes to adopt them. I had sort of dreaded the announcement, fearing their refusal. On the contrary, they were both delighted at the prospect. In the darkness they both told me the long story. I was not prepared for what I heard, and will not relate all of it. They were both abused. Bunny by one of her cousins and Swift Antelope by an uncle. They had been beaten on numerous occasions and the story went on and on. I had to listen, knowing that what I heard would help Dakota and I both to try and set their lives straight.

I held both of them close, closer than any one in my life. I knew beyond a shadow of a doubt that I loved them . I knew then and there that I would never let any one take them from us. At that, a long low howl came from somewhere off to my right. I knew that the spirit dogs approved.

Dakota had the bed and her sister cleaned up. I was glad that I could have my bed back for the night and Dakota's sister was sleeping it off over in the corner bunk. The rest of the night went without incident.

Morning came with the usual chores and a big breakfast. Their mother ate nothing. She looked like a ghost as she sat at the other end of the table. Dakota must have poured a half gallon of coffee into her as she tried to get her to eat. Sam kept looking at his watch as if expecting to get out of there in the next instant. Finally Sparkling Water spoke. "I need a drink. I need one bad." My first thought was to go to the medicine cabinet and pour her a stiff one. Dakota ever my mind reader shook her head , no. "I need a drink, and I want one now." She started for the door. Dakota called to her, "You wont get far, you are over a hundred miles from Fairbanks and you will freeze to death." She sat down and as if in a sudden flash of reality said, "Fairbanks? Isn't that up North? How did I get here?" I, in my ever present wisdom said, "You're a drunk and." I was suddenly interrupted by Sam.

"You are here to see your children. I am the one that sent you the letters concerning the adoption of your children by your sister and her husband Paul." Suddenly she seemed to face the situation as she broke down in tears. I thought, oh crap, a crying jag. As clear as crystal she began to speak. " I know that I am a drunk. I know that I am not a fit mother. It is Dakota that should have had these children. I cant take care of them, I never could." She looked right at the kids and in the coldest words I could imagine said "I don't want you, I never wanted you."

I could feel the pain, the pain of total rejection. The look in the eyes of Bunny and Swift Antelope should never be seen by any one. The hurt had to have sunk deep into their being. Dakota took them in her arms and the three of them wept. I have to give their mother credit for one thing. She asked Sam for a pen. Sam had the papers in front of him as he guided her to the place to sign. In a shaking scrawl she gave the kids to us.

Sam said that he would have to present it to the judge but felt that we would have no problems. No sooner had he spoke and Dave dropped onto the strip and quicker than I can write this they were off. There were no good byes and no tears.

A week later found us in Fairbanks for the funeral and the judges opinion. The story had a sad and a happy ending. Sparkling Water in a promise to Sam that she would stay in her hotel room until he picked her up, hit the bars of Fairbanks. She was found the next morning on the banks of the river frozen solid.

Chapter 26

Family Lessons

There remained little snow of the previous winter. Just enough to operate the snow machine one more time. The kids said little as we flew home. Once we put the Cessna away Swift Antelope jumped on his machine and flew down the strip like he was going to take off. He rounded the end of the strip and sped by us at a vengeance. A hard left and he hit Moms old trail as the sound of his machine disappeared.

Dakota commented about his present mental state. I assured her that he would be back soon. I had no fear that he would go to far and do something rash. I knew that he would soon be out of gas and would have to walk back home.

Sure enough, an hour later he came in the door. Dakota had prepared a quick supper after I stoked the old stove. Bunny sat looking out the window seemingly a million miles away.

"Lets eat", Dakota exclaimed as we all sat down to another fine meal. The kids were understandably silent. " Hold it there Swift Antelope, before you stick that fork into that piece of meat, lets pray." I don't know what I had said that prompted it but both started to weep. I went ahead, "Father we thank you for this food but more than that, we thank you for this family. Father I give my word to these kids that they will always be our family. With your help they will grow up to be as you want them to be. Amen, lets eat." Dakota got up from the table long enough to get the judges order. The kids had not been present at the hearing so had no idea what transpired. Dakota read the order and names therein. Bunny McAuffe and Swift Antelope McAuffe. It took a long minute but suddenly it started to sink in. "McAuffe? You mean that we are adopted?" From Bunny, then Swift Antelope. "Swift Antelope McAuffe, Swift Antelope McAuffe." He repeated over and over. I knew it hadn't sunk in, so just sat back with my coffee and relished the moment. It would hit them soon. The realization that they had a new life and a new identity.

To my surprise nothing else was said that evening as well as the next morning. The lessons for the day went as usual with one exception. They both turned in their papers to Dakota signed Bunny McAuffe and Swift Antelope McAuffe. Dakota showed me the papers and I smiled.

Swift Antelope and I serviced the snow machines and put them in the hanger for the summer. The snow had left with the coming of the sun. We had just finished for the day when I heard it. "What are we going to do next dad?" It took a little thought at what he had just said but then I just smiled and said,"dad and his son are going to learn how to fly." You would have thought I gave him the moon. You could see the excitement, feel its pulse. "Well we have covered most of the pre flight school that you need so it's about time, you earned it."

At supper he couldn't contain him self as he told Dakota and Bunny what he was going to do. "Oh no you don't, not with out me." Bunny was not going to be left out. I had no plans for that and told her that they would have to take turns and really concentrate on the lessons. She turned toward Dakota and exclaimed dad's going to teach me how to fly." There it was again, music to my ears, dad.

I think Dakota tried to play a little joke on them as she said, "You know that you have to learn at the duel controls, don't you?" They said "Well yes we guess." The Cessna has the only duel controls and I own the Cessna. So what are you supposed to say?" Both piped up "please, please, pretty please mom." Now it was Dakota's turn to hear the words. Words that make the heart melt, words that will get you almost anything, mom.

They had done well with their lessons for the school year and passed all their exams. My next proclamation had to be "Schools out for the summer." I knew we would get a hug for that one.

The next day they woke in anticipation of a day of flying. They reminded me of my self when I secretly learned to fly. I couldn't wait to get in the air. "Whose first?" Wrong question as they started one of their old battles. Dakota pulled out a coin and tossed it high in the air. "call it Bunny." Bunny screamed "heads." Tails came down in a final spin. Swift Antelope couldn't contain himself as he stuck his tongue out at her. I popped him on the butt and said "lets fly."

"Come on Bunny, us girls will do something else for the time being." Swift Antelope and I ran the pre flight check and he took the left seat. I had the controls as I told him to put his hands on the yoke and his feet on the peddles. "Lightly now, I want you to feel what I am doing." I told him to start her up. The engine roared to life as we watched the engine temperature come up. We taxied out to the strip and made a left turn. I looked over to see one happy boy concentrating to the best of his ability. "Run her up." He throttled her up and we began our take off roll. Down the strip and at the last instant I pulled her up. I could feel his hands on the controls almost match mine. Once in the air we circled a couple of times and headed out toward the haul road. We leveled off at 3000 feet and I took my hands off the yoke, at the same time looking out the corner of my eye. Sheer horror on his part, I grinned. We flew around for about an hour, doing one maneuver after another. "OK take her back." I wanted to see if he had been paying attention to his location. Was he lost? No problem, he banked to the right and made a full turn and laid her right on course for home. This kid was a natural like his old man. I let him bring her in with only a slight assist form me. We did a couple of light bounces as we glided to a stop and he spun her around. "There dad, how's that, got her pointing in the right direction for Bunny."

We had an early lunch, then Bunny and I went up. I felt that she had a better handle on the controls than Swift Antelope. She had a lighter touch, kind of like a woman's touch, nice and gentle. She would also make a good pilot. She was so good that I kept my hands completely off the controls on the entire landing. No pucker factor, perfect.

Swift Antelope was ready for another go. This time Dakota took him up and Bunny and I did father daughter things. Bunny poured a cup for me and gave me one of the sweet rolls that her and her mom had made.

"You know Dad, I didn't think I would like living here. I didn't want to leave my friends. I was wrong. I have learned more here than I would ever have on the Rosebud. I am glad that you are my dad, I never knew one before. I am learning a lot about things. Thank you."

She went on to say some other mushy stuff but still the word dad won my heart.

It wasn't long and Dakota and Swift Antelope were back. Bunny ran to the strip and her and Dakota ran another pre flight and re fueled the bird. In no time they were in the air as I watched them turn to the Northwest.

That night at supper I gave each one of them their own log book and told them that I didn't know if the inspectors would accept it, but keep track of your hours anyway.

Bunny's birthday came and went. Swift Antelope was not far behind. Now they were old enough to get their license. Bunny at seventeen, could get her license but Swift Antelope could only get his student license at sixteen. I know this did not set well with his warrior ego, but that's life.

We all made the trip to our home in Fairbanks and soon days were spent in gaining flying hours. Each required forty hours of total flying time. Ten hours were required out of the forty as solo time and five of those were cross country. We pushed for all we could, to get the time in over a two week period. Dakota used her Cessna for Bunny and as all the aircraft of our company were tied up, we rented a Cessna from one of our friends, for Swift Antelope.

The written and oral exams were passed by both kids and Bunny passed her practical exam with kudos from the examiner. Poor Swift Antelope put everything he had into the project but was very disappointed that he had to wait a year for his license.

There were the usual visits with all the family. The grand kids had grown like weeds. Dinners at the home place were great affairs with Ladonna and Bunny doing most of the cooking. After Swift Antelope finished all he could to get his permit, he took to flying with Dave as space permitted. Dave let him take the controls of the Otter on more than one occasion. I spent a great deal of time with Joe.

Poor Joe, still able to take care of the house and the daughters, but getting slower in his speech and actions. "You, know, dad, I, am, not, getting, any, better. I, know, I, will, never, get, in, the, air, again." My heart once again broke. What could I do but pray.

We all grew restless to return to the cabin. There is only so much town that I can take. The return trip found the Cessna loaded with as much weight as we could carry. Even though Bunny still did not have the permit to carry passengers, Dakota gave the controls to her. She flew like a professional. Swift Antelope sat with me, sullen look and all.

Home never looked so good, as Bunny laid her in right on target, taxied to the cabin and shut her down. Dakota and I told her how proud of her we were but Swift Antelope kicked up the dust as he headed to the cabin, with out a word.

While we busied our selves putting away the goods that we brought from town, the sound of the Cub barked to life. Oh crap I thought as I rushed to the door only to see my bird taxing for take off. Before I could get out a feeble stop, it was in the air. "I'm going to tan his hide when and if he gets back. Dakota you see that? Who in the hell does he think he is? Where's my dam shot gun?" I of course knew that a shot gun was not the answer as well as I knew that I would never use it on him or my plane.

"Come on back in here Paul. If I recall you learned to fly at thirteen and you didn't even have a permit or a teacher." My dander was riled up. "I had the best teacher I know of, myself. That's not even his own plane. At least I owned my own plane." Dakota gave me a big squeeze and said, "Now Paul."

Bunny thought it great sport. She silently relished the thought of the wrath that her brother would face. She started singing "he's going to get it, he's going to get it." "That's enough Bunny." Dakota admonished.

It was only thirty minutes but seemed like a day before we heard the Cub on final. I ran to the door to see Swift Antelope glide in for a perfect landing. Pride, no matter what the reason, did not take the place of my planned vengeance.

A large smile from a small kid greeted me half way to the door. "Don't grin at me young man, or should I say stupid man, get your butt out to the hanger. I'll deal with you in a minute."

Dakota's famous words for everything, attacked my ears. "Now Paul." "Don't now Paul me, he's got to learn a lesson." I could hear Dakota's last words as I swiftly walked to the hanger. "Remember Paul, what did your dad do?" That took the wind out of my sails. Dad was proud of me.

I never said a word to him, except to come to supper. Calmer now that I had a piece of steak in my mouth, I said "your grounded." He started to say something but I continued. "Your not grounded because you flew. Your grounded because you stole my plane. It's as bad as horse theven in the old days. You don't go around the North country stealing someone's transportation." I took a glance toward Bunny, then to Dakota, then winked. Finished with him for the time being I said to Bunny, "you, young lady, can use the Cub any time you want, till further notice."

Chapter 27

The Kids meet the Spirits

Bunny wasted no time taking me up on my offer. Swift Antelope was relegated to the task of aircraft service manager. I thought I was kidding when I gave him the title but he took the job seriously. As I went out the door and down to the hanger, I could see him washing away on the Cub. By the time I arrived he informed me that all checked out and she was ready to fly. I thought he may have been pulling a fast one, so inspected her for my self. Sure enough, all was in order. Before I could complement him he turned to Dakota's Cessna. I let the complement ride and went back to the cabin shaking my head. This boy never ceases to amaze me. Dakota and Bunny poured over a map. Bunny had her route planed for the day and Dakota's blessing to go. Bunny turned and asked if it was OK. I nodded and said something like, if it's OK with your mother it's OK with me.

Fifteen minutes later she was airborne, leaving Swift Antelope washing the Cessna and glancing in her direction. I could feel the hurt in him but had to stick to my guns and carry out the sentence.

Three minutes later, Dakota came running, screaming that Bunny had forgotten her map. Worried that Bunny would become lost, Dakota turned frantic. To me there were two options, one, Bunny would realize her error and return soon, two, one of us would have to chase after her and bring her back. Dakota wanted to go at once. I opted for the first choice. "Bunny is no dummy, she will be back." We waited for fifteen or twenty minutes and sure enough, a speck on the horizon appeared. Besides acute embarrassment all turned out well. She returned to the air.

I waited late into the evening. No Bunny. She had told us that she planned on a flight to Fairbanks, just to get used to the route. She should have been back. Now it was I who had all kinds of thoughts. Was she down? Was she off course and down? Did she miss Fairbanks altogether and down some place beyond? I thought of the time that we searched for so long for Ladonna. I thought of all the close scrapes that I had over the years. How could I be so stupid and let my daughter fly so young? What was I thinking? I paced up and down the strip, until Dakota sent Swift Antelope to bring me in for supper. I couldn't eat. Dakota for once seemed calm. I finally resolved to take Swift Antelope with me as spotter. We needed to find out what had happened.

While we pre flighted the Cessna, Bunny appeared low on the horizon. Another very smooth landing. Bunny hopped out of the Cub. After the big hug, the next question had to be, "where have you been?" I should have been furious, however I found that I could not be furious with this girl. "Well dad, I made the flight to Fairbanks and Dave refueled the Cub. Ladonna and Joe had me to dinner and Ladonna and I just had to do some shopping. By the time we got back I knew that I would be late getting back. Rather than have you worry, I took off and set course for home. The flight went smooth and I loved it. The country approaching the mountains is so beautiful. I love to fly dad. At that I got a big hug. Now how is a dad supposed to be angry after that perfectly good explanation? "By the way dad, I saw a big white dog crossing a sand bar not too far from here. There was a woman with a red blanket wrapped around her. I did a sharp bank to take another look for her but she disappeared. I cant figure out what they were doing way out there. There are no roads or houses and I couldn't see a trail.

After supper, I sat at the table with a cup of coffee in one hand and a tooth pick in the other. This would be as good a time as any to bring the subject up. I got up and got the old tin box. Laying the box on the table, I opened it. Swift Antelope and Bunny both asked what I had in the box. The first item out was the manuscript of Skipping Rock that my dad wrote. Dakota coughed as I blew some imaginary dust off of it. Must have been the musty smell of old paper. Next I removed the bound Copy of the finished book that I put together so many years before. Eyes widened as I pulled out the old pocket watch, the velvet bag, and a few other treasures. Swift Antelope's jaw dropped as I pulled out the knife that Charlie Two Bears had made for my dad.

I went through a brief history of the items before I placed them back in the box. All, that is, except the manuscript and the published copy. "Here Bunny, take your pick, this is the family history as told by my dad. You can ether read one copy or the other." Bunny looked first at one than the other and picked the manuscript. I handed the bound copy to Swift Antelope. "I think this is as good as time as any for you both to learn about your new family."

As the kids found their favorite reading spot, I looked at Dakota and said "They can read my partial manuscript of McAuffe's Arctic when they are finished.

I think Bunny regretted picking the old manuscript. I found dad's writing difficult to decipher when I edited it for the final book. Swift Antelope read the parts he liked best aloud to Dakota and I. It was a treat to see his excitement. His reading skill improved by the day. Bunny impressed by the apparent great cooking by Angelene, wished that she had her recipes.

They eventually got to Paul and Rachael's saga. Swift Antelope loved the bow contest story. I saw the light go on in Bunny as she tried to put two and two together. "Dad, Rachael, dressed in the red blanket, appears similar to the woman I saw the other day."

That's all it took. In an instant, there, setting on the bear skin, two magnificent dogs. Swift Antelope, about fell out of his chair as he said "holy cat's." I thought Bunny would faint. Dakota just smiled and approached the dogs. Bunny, Swift Antelope, meet Spirit and "... Just then Rachael appeared, wrapped in the red blanket. Bunny did faint for an instant. Swift Antelope's jaw dropped a foot. Dakota finished her introduction. "Kids, this is Rachael, Spirit and Broken Eye."

"Your kidding, surly your kidding. You are kidding aren't you Mom?" Rachael spoke, "no kidding kids. Sorry for the intrusion but I thought it as good a time as any."

Bunny and Swift Antelope just sat starring at the spectacle. A long minute passed and Dakota quietly asked if Rachael would like tea. "Oh yes, I always look forward to your tea. I jumped up to stoke the stove and put the kettle on. The kids, said not a word. Rachael spoke. "I know you are dying to pet the dogs, go ahead, they wont bite."

Swift Antelope approached them carefully. Suddenly Broken Eye lunged at him and pinned him to the floor. Spirit followed, Tuk jumped in on top. A free for all followed. Swift Antelope sat up with an arm around the neck of each dog. "Now that's what I call dogs!" You could almost sense the rejection as Tuk jumped into my lap. "That's alright Tuk, I know you are a great dog." as I stroked his fur.

Rachael sat upright and sipped her tea. Speaking softly, words that Bunny and Swift Antelope needed to hear. 'You know kids, I am here only because God wants me here. I am not quite an angel, nor am I human, at least not now. How ever I am related to you. I am as related to you as much as I am related to this man that has taken you in but I might be more related to Dakota."

Now she had my interest and I could see Dakota leaning ever more forward, hanging on Rachael's every word. "This man Paul Rachael, your adoptive father is related to Paul, the man I married in the 1600's. That's a long time ago, isn't it?" The kids nodded.

I quietly got up and poured her another cup of tea. "A friend of mine and myself escaped from our English captors only to find Paul laying in a pool of his own blood. Well I wont go into that as you can read the story for your self." Bunny suddenly, as though a flash bulb had gone off said. "I just finished that story in dad's book. Did all that really happen?" "Yes Bunny and more than that. There are parts to the story that were never known or told. That's why I am here. I want to tell you more of the tale." Rachael once again disappeared. The kids disappointed though they were, seemed to understand.

Dakota told them of her experiences with Rachael and suggested that they try and get a good nights sleep. "I am sure that sometime soon, when you least expect it, Rachael will be back." "That's not fair" Bunny replied, "How can I sleep when things are just getting interesting?"

I should have asked the same question. I laid awake until who knows when. I finally awoke to the ever tantalizing aroma of meat in the skillet and coffee boiling over. Humming quietly and bending over the stove, stood Rachael. I should be used to her intrusions by now. I ask, where is the privacy when some spirit is constantly in and out of your life. Spirit or no spirit I eased out of bed trying not to wake Dakota. I stepped over the three dogs and went out side.

When I came back in, Rachael handed me a cup and I sat down at the table. I watched her for a long minute while she deftly turned the meat. My eyes ran around the old room. The kids still slumbered away and Dakota as yet made not a move. Rachael sat down next to me, keeping one eye on the stove and one on the dogs. She spoke. "The dogs look very peaceful." She went on, "Look at the little one snuggled between the others. He is protected and he knows it." I thought her to go on but once again and just as fast she disappeared.

"Dam I wish she wouldn't do that" I exclaimed as Dakota stuck her head out from the covers. "Do what?" I replied to Dakota that Rachael had just fixed breakfast and took off with out a word. "Better get the kids up and eat before it gets cold." I said, as I went to wake them.

We didn't say any thing to the kids about Rachael's visit. They commented several times over the next weeks about her absence. There remained nothing more that I could tell them that would explain it. Winter returned and we settled back into our routine.

Chapter 28

The Old People

It was about 20 above as a light snow fell. Supper over, I continued to write the manuscript of the "Five Pipers". Dakota puttered with some thing as the kids read. Tuk, lay in my lap dreaming dreams that only dogs can fathom. I thought I had heard a drum beat. Far off in the distance, not the type of drum as the Pipers had in the story but different. The sound faded and I wondered about it as I went back to writing. The sound returned. No, I was sure of it this time. It wasn't the drums of the story I wrote about. It sounded more like the drums of native peoples. I was completely familiar with the drums of the arctic. These were not the same.

"Do you hear that?" "Hear what?" Dakota said. " I think I hear drums." "Come on Paul, I don't hear drums. Do you hear drums kids?" By this time chuckles came from every one but me. "Now I know a drum when I hear one." "Yes Paul we know you know what a drum sounds like. Didn't you tell me that you were going to write something about the drums of the Pipers?" "Yes Dakota but these are different." "Yes, yes Paul." was all Dakota said.

Another hour or so passed as I kept the sound of the drums to myself. I noticed first Dakota then Bunny kind of tapping their fingers to some unseen rhythm. Then Swift Antelope spoke. "Who are you?" The rest of us looked up at once. I saw nothing as Dakota stood and moved toward Bunny. "Who are you?" Swift Antelope repeated. Suddenly I could see five old people, dressed in animal skins, setting on the floor. Three held ancient looking drums that they beat in unison. Rachael appeared with her usual apology for the intrusion. She held her finger to her lips as if to keep us quiet. After a time, the sounds slowed to a halt. Rachael introduced the most ancient person I had ever seen.

I would like for you to meet Uncoa. The drums started again, this time very quietly. I couldn't help but recall the drummer at Point

Hope. The old man spoke. His voice feeble, his eyes sunken with age. " I am Uncoa, story teller to the people. I am the son of your grand father's, grandfather's, grandfather." I quickly tried to calculate how far back this sent him in time. I soon forgot to count as he laid his thin hands on each of Swift Antelope's shoulders. "You will also be a story teller. All but one of these people with me are the same. It is our life, we keep the history alive. In your case something happened to your family after the white men killed that generation at Wounded Knee. We can no longer let the history lay in silence."

"Philippe and Annette the woman known to the people as the twin, lived to the North of the big lakes in the Canada of today. Annette gave Philippe three sons and two daughters. Both daughters and one son died with their mother from small pox. Many people died but not Philippe or the two sons." The drums went silent as Rachael spoke. "Philippe was my son, Swift Antelope. He was adopted like you, but that mattered none at all. I missed him for many years."

The drums started slowly as the old man resumed his tale. "Philippe was angry, more angry than any one had ever seen. He lived with the people for several more years and eventually took a new wife. I am the first son of Philippe and Ta. Philippe took his new wife and me away from all the people. He wanted nothing to do with the enemy. The enemy of that time was both French and the English. He moved his family West across Canada and settled with the mountain people. These stories have been told over many campfires and in many winter lodges. Philippe was an old man when he died. I was about thirty winters old when he died. People say he just died of a broken heart for Ta. I know it was not long after that when he died. I took a wife who was one of several that had been captured in one of our many wars with the Crow People of the South. She did not love me but I wanted her. I gave three ponies for her and oh yes I also had to throw in two dogs." The drums stopped the moment he stopped. We sat bug eyed and all ears as the drums laid out a slow rhythmic beat once again, as a second man spoke. " I am the great grand son of this man Uncoa. He lived a good life and had many sons from the woman who did not love him. I was born in Alberta. We moved with the seasons. We were free. When we traveled with our family from the south we had nothing but trouble. That is why we lived the cold winters in Canada. The soldiers of the south killed our family every chance they had. They allowed all the buffalo to be killed. They along with other white men took our land and took our way of life slowly from us. We thought we would be OK if we signed their treaties but it was no good. My sons son became a Lakota. He fought in many small battles but was eventually sent to Pine ridge when the white man got control." Once again the drums stopped when the man stopped talking.

Rachael asked if we could have some tea. Dakota jumped up and I followed on her heels telling Rachael how sorry I was for my bad manners. I stoked up the fire while Dakota, hardly able to take her eyes off of the old people, prepared the tea. We quickly heated some of the left over moose and served the group. They ate in silence, pouring lavish amounts of sugar into their tea and wiping the moose grease from their mouths with their sleeves. Grunts of satisfaction went around the group.

The third person to speak, spoke with out the drums. At first I had thought it to be a man but soon found an old woman speaking in a soft loving voice. "I want you Dakota to know that I am not a story teller. I am your grand mother. The one that you never knew. I am a healer. You take after me. You are guided by my prayers. Seek the knowledge that you need and it will be given you by Our Father in Heaven. Blessed are the healers, they are Gods servants. They are the ones that many times stand between good and evil, life and death. You are from a long line of healers spanning time and space. Some are healers, some are story tellers, some are both. Swift Antelope you could be both. It is up to you to seek your guide and carry your burden. Bunny, some are called to serve others in different ways. You will have to find your guide in your dreams. Listen to the wind and the hawk."

Silence swept the room, no one moved for the longest time. Finally the old woman spoke once more. "Paul we hope that we have given you some further grasp of your place in our family. Your relationship with Rachael is our relationship. We are one."

How could I say anything? I knew the one story and now I knew some of the other. The circle was drawing closer. I could see now that over time all people were related in one way or another.

The old woman drew closer to Bunny and laid her hand on her, then moved to Swift Antelope and did the same. A shudder could be seen in Swift Antelope as he dropped to the floor in a dead faint. At that, the entire group melted into obscurity.

Swift Antelope lay on the bear skin rug, out cold. Panic ran through me as I thought thoughts of death or coma. Dakota sat with him cradling his head in her lap. "Dakota, aren't you the least concerned?" I said ,thinking that we should take him to the doctor in Fairbanks. She just kept stroking his long black hair and rocked back and forth. I could hear some tune that she hummed but could not identify it.

The clock ticked on the wall and Bunny just stared into space seemingly oblivious to every thing. One hour passed ,than two. My concern turned to my stomach and I said so. Suddenly as I spoke Bunny jumped up and started rattling pans. It must have been the sound because Swift Antelope woke with a start.

The meal that night tasted great. God, that girl could cook. Dakota and Swift Antelope didn't talk much during the meal and I could see that Bunny wanted to say something but couldn't or wouldn't.

Finally unable to stand it any longer I asked Bunny to talk to me. She broke into tears. Tears streamed down her face in torrents. What have I done, I thought.

She began slowly, words born between sobs. I listened intently but could hardly make out what she said. I reached across the table and took her hand. "Bunny, slow down, relax, it will come." A long pause, "dad the old people seemed to have something for my brother but nothing for me". I simply pressed her hand a little firmer." Bunny, I don't know what to say right now, lets wait a little and see if we get an answer." I really had no idea what to tell her, than I said "Bunny didn't the old woman say that you had to seek your dream in the hawk and the wind?" She looked at me for a long while and said that she was tired, in several minutes she lay sound asleep across my bed.

Swift Antelope had a different air about him. Usually fairly quiet, he became more so. Days passed and both kids, though still interested in school work seemed lost in thought.

Dakota thought she might have a solution and privately shared her ideas. "Paul, I think that Swift Antelope will grow up to be someone special. Not that Bunny wont but he will fulfill some special place in his peoples history." I had no idea that she thought that way. "What makes you say that?" "Paul, I listen to my own spirit and it seems possible that I am supposed to lead Swift Antelope in a direction that we haven't thought of before. I want to take him to Anaktuvuk Village. There is some one there that I met ,that might be able to help.

"What about Bunny?" Seemed like a fair question to me. "Paul I think you have the question of Bunny, well in hand." "What do you mean?" Dakota hit me in my favorite spot with her next words. "Do you like to eat Paul?" "Yes, you know I do." Than the idea of a possible answer, took flight and I winked at my beloved wife. How wise of her.

That night as we rested in each other's arms we talked of our plans. Dakota would take Swift Antelope to the village and I would work on my idea for Bunny.

Chapter 29

Empty Cabin

December, seemingly the coldest and I know the darkest time of year above the Arctic Circle. Dakota and Swift Antelope took off in the dark with the temperature at 47 below. I did not and still don't think that flying at that temperature is the smartest thing to do. I felt it very unwise but couldn't stand up to Dakota's reasoning. Why is it that the folly of our youth always seems to come back and haunt us? I can hear her now. "Well Paul it seems that you have told me enough stories of your exploits in the cold. Were those just tales of bravado or don't you think that I can handle my self?" I had to admit that I have flown for a lifetime in such extremes and that ended any hope of talking her out of it.

She only planned to drop Swift Antelope off with her friend and visit for a short time. I thought her due back in a minimum of three days. Five days past, still no Dakota. Bunny reminded me that after all, the thermometer out side said 68 below. I checked it by the hour until it read 72 below at 4 AM. When Bunny woke to the sounds of my rummaging around and complained in a strong voice, I realized that Dakota was being prudent.

"Who you writing to dad?" "I am writing to Ian and Peggy, not that its any of your business." " Well aren't we getting testy." "Its not that girl, I'm on edge over this weather and your mother's delay." That was true but I had a special favor to ask of Ian and Peggy. I stood positive that they would go along with my idea. I stuffed the letter in the envelope, looked in the address book for their address and finished, laid it on the table.

Bunny and I busied our selves with chores, eating, more chores and more eating. If she only knew of my idea.

On the 23rd the temperature modified to the low twenties below zero. LaDonna slipped in long enough to drop off supplies, have a meal and put up a Christmas tree. Every thing was fine with the family except for Joe, who slipped more in his memory every day. Dear Joe how I hoped for my boy.

I gave the letter to Ladonna and asked her to put the best postage on it and send it off straight away.

Dakota returned on the morning of the twenty fourth. The temperature had modified even more and it was a balmy 10 below. She left Swift Antelope in the care of the village health aide and said that she cried all the way back home. Dakota kept telling me that she thought it best. She hoped that he would find some thing special in the people of that far off village that would help him in his quest for his future.

Swift Antelope or no Swift Antelope we had to get ready for Christmas. The tree stood in it's usual spot and Dakota decorated it and the cabin in a festive mood. Bunny baked. She baked from morning till night. I had the honor of tasting all the samples of her ability as they came out of the oven. The aroma, God the aroma of baked goods of every description. It seemed that I drank gallons of coffee. The sacrifices a father must make. She stuffed me with cookies and cakes till I thought I would bust, then told me to save room for the up coming Christmas dinner.

Christmas morning broke cold and clear. Cold yes, but only 5 below. "Lets go for a ride, it's perfect for the snow machines".

Not much coaching needed to get the girls on their machines. Rooster tails as usual being all I saw as I brought up the rear. We rode for the better part of four hours before heading back home. The sky was clear in the low light of mid morning. Even though 10 Am head lights sparkled off of new fallen snow. Ladonna buzzed us heading for the cabin. She had already landed and off loaded her family as well as Joe and Caroline.

We gathered around the table in thanks for all that we had. We did our best to recall the meaning of Christmas. Without Father Paddy and some of the others I had difficulty getting into the spirit of the day. That is until Ladonna told me of the phone call. That did it for me. I could now give Bunny what I thought she would like the most.

I banged a spoon on a glass and made my big announcement. "Ladies and gentlemen, not being one for long words." Joe interrupted

"B,a,l,o,n,e,y". I gave him a sideways glance in fake mockery. It really broke my heart this time to see how far he had gone down hill. "I continue, Bunny I am pleased to announce your gift, please stand up and take a bow for all the great food that you have put out for us." The small group, knowing what was in store for Bunny applauded wildly. Embarrassed, Bunny stood. "Bunny your mother and I have made arrangements for you to go to Scotland and live with Ian and Peggy for a while. Peggy wants to put you through the remainder of high school and have you work with her in the five star restaurant she manages. In addition she wants to sponsor you to the best culinary school in the Isles." Every one cheered as Bunny stood in amazement then threw herself into our arms. "Dad, Mom, I, I, I never dreamed that this would be possible. How did you know? How did you know that I have dreamed of being a chef for months?"

Dakota looked at me for words. With tears of happiness I said, "Well sweetie It hasn't been too difficult to see that all the food you have prepared for all of us, was prepared with love. To watch you in all aspects of cooking is always a treat." Dakota chimed in, "There are a lot of things that you could do. You are an intelligent young woman. We just think that this may be what you are supposed to do. You will have to decide for your self. Aunt Peggy is willing to help and I am sure she loves you and will see that you are well taken care of. We will miss you. Oh God, how we will miss you."

The rest of the holiday felt festive. Gifts galore and time spent with my family couldn't have been better. Dakota and Bunny wasted no time getting Bunnies belongings together. She was to spend time in Fairbanks with Ladonna shopping of course and getting her passport in order. They scurried around the cabin packing this and unpacking that until all appeared in order.

As fast as the holiday appeared, it passed. Tearful goodbyes, loving kisses and long warnings and do's and don'ts for Bunny and before I knew it they were all gone.

I slumped down in my chair and felt the loneliness. I still had my beloved Dakota but this time it was not the same. No Bunny dancing through her kitchen work and no Swift Antelope to bug me with his countless questions. The twins were growing so fast. They clung to me at every turn. Joe worried me. Ladonna said that Dave missed us but remained too busy to take the Holiday off. The rest of the family was doing fine and no need for concern.

Christmas night came early. The temperature again dropped to fifty or so below. I didn't look at the old thermometer, I could just tell by the way the trees popped and snapped. Dakota lay curled up in her favorite spot wrapped in a new robe that Ladonna had made. I stoked the stove and got it to that spot where it always starts to chug. I knew the sound well. Warmth made war on the cold attempting to invade our space.

I passed a cup of coffee to Dakota and laid a plate of Bunnies delectable creations on her side table. We both cried.

Chapter 30

New Beginnings

In the dead of winter the days were almost indistinguishable from nights. only the faint light of pre dawn gave hint of new beginnings to come in the spring. The ever present chugging of the stove continued its war with the cold. Chores were short. The planes remained in the old hanger and we reveled in the quiet. Occasionally short jaunts on the snow machines broke the silence of another arctic night. We played poker, with Dakota most always winning. If I recall, by mid winter I was in the hole about ten thousand dollars to her. Dakota took up writing, Tuk ever present in her lap. I thought her a good writer but who am I to say. She penned her stories much as my dad did. Her hand, much finer than dad's, and easy to read. Dakota had a grasp on story telling, a gift as far as I was concerned. The title, "Sioux Winter". At first I thought she might be writing short essays but as each day passed, I could see a full fledged book emerging from her pages. It had to be in the family blood, so many story tellers.

I continued writing the story of the "Five Pipers", mixed with reading. I easily slipped back into the habit of prayer. Contemplation on the mysteries of faith deepened with feelings of understanding.

One minute the sounds of winter and the next the sounds of an approaching aircraft. We didn't expect any one, Dave was not due with supplies for two or three weeks.

The plane circled several times, enough time for us to throw on our gear and get out side. One more round of the cabin and the sound faded to the South. Strange I thought, as we turned to go back in. The plane returned with a faint rumble of it's engine. Slowly it came into sight, lined up with the end of the strip. The pilot wasted no runway as he dropped on the very end of the strip, skies throwing snow in a cloud. He kept the power on until the very end than cut it. The small plane sank up to it's belly in the unpacked field.

Swift Antelope wasted no time jumping out. He dropped through the thin crust of snow and sank to his hips. Mom, Dad, he called as he plowed his way toward us. He fell exhausted into our open arms as we saw the pilot emerge. He was a short man, no more than five feet. I could see his long gray hair flowing over his parka ruff. He waded in the tracks left by Swift Antelope and threw out his bare right hand in a hardy hello. "Vernon White Wolf, Vern for short."

We wasted no time covering his plane and draining the oil. That done, we went into the cabin to a pot of Dakota's steaming coffee. Vern sat at the table next to the stove, hands wrapped around a mug. Swift Antelope could not get enough hugs from mom as she hurriedly prepared the noon meal a little early. "Watch it now boy you will get burned" came from Dakota. I could tell her lack of sincerity as she hugged him back just as much. Vern grinned from ear to ear as he spoke. "That boy hugs my wife almost as much." "Another cup?" I asked, thinking of offering a wee shot of rum but deciding against it. "Don't mind if I do" he retorted, asking if I had a wee shot of rum. "Just to take the chill off a bit."

It was obvious that Vern was full blooded Inuit, short as I said, round of body with teeth broken and missing with years of use. I judged his age to be about fifty but it was hard to tell. He had three fingers missing on his left hand and the same elbow appeared bent in an odd direction.

"So, what brings both of you out on this cold day?" Vernon started to speak but Swift Antelope interrupted. "We were out spotting Caribou and came so close to home, that I begged him to stop in." Dakota chided Swift Antelope for interrupting, as Vernon White Wolf spoke.

"He is always impatient to tell a story. When we gather in the meeting house, Swift Antelope always has something to say. He is a good story teller. He has told us of your family stories and I wanted to meet you. He didn't have to beg too hard to get me to stop by."

Dakota laid out a fine spread . We all dove into it with abandon. Vern helped him self to a big moose rib just as I was about to latch onto it. "Don't worry boys, there are more where that came from." Dakota chimed in. Drippings ran down Vern's chin as Dakota slid a big rib onto my plate. "Good, Good food, the food of the people is always good. Not like the store bought food we ship in from Fairbanks." I had to agree as we both tried to out eat one another. Swift Antelope ate till I thought he would bust. I noticed he had grown taller and must have gained thirty pounds.

After supper we all sat around the table, that is except for Tuk and Swift Antelope. Tuk had his little teeth wrapped around a rib bone, happy as a puppy in mud. Swift Antelope, laid on the big Bear rug. Occasionally moans and groans came from his direction. "Serves him right" I said, as Vern nodded agreement.

Stories of hunting, stories of cold and stories of both families were told into the late evening. The smell of hot apple pie pierced the door of the oven and teased our nostrils. I could tell Vern waited in anticipation, as I did for the first bite.

Early the next morning we dug out his plane and fired up the heat under his engine. We then packed the runway with the snow machines. Swift Antelope did a good pre flight check and before we could say more, they were off into the pre dawn darkness.

Every time we have visitors, there is a feeling of loss when they leave. I could understand our feelings for Swift Antelope but not really the feeling of loss when Vern left.

"What do you think of Vern, Dakota?" "What on Earth do you mean, he's a nice, pleasant fellow as far as fellows go." "No Dakota, I mean did you see something special in him?" "Not especially Paul, why do you ask?" "Well sweety, I think we will see a lot more of him." "How so Paul? You only just met him."

I could not get the meeting of Vernon White Wolf out of my mind. We had no sooner settled back into our routine when another aircraft came in the next day. This time it was Dave. Dave swung his plane around, cut the engine, hopped out and as we put the bird to bed, asked who had been there.

I told him of our visit with Swift Antelope and meeting Vern White Wolf. Dave's reply startled me. "Dad don't you remember him?" I had to admit that I hadn't. "Vernon White Wolf is the owner of White Wolf Aviation. He's the one who picked you up after your crash. Vern operates his small service out of Anaktuvuk Village. Surly you must know him, you two have been flying up here all your lives." I had to scratch my head over that one. How could I forget someone in the same business? Especially some one who had rescued me. I puzzled over that and wondered why Vern had not mentioned the rescue.

It was good to see Dave again. It was I who paid far too little attention to this son. Dave was the rock on which our business grew. While we talked over supper he jumped up and went for his coat. Now what is he up to I thought. "I almost forgot, mail." He laid it on the table and I quickly rummaged through it. Bills and contracts of one form or another. In the middle of the stack a letter with postage from Scotland. "A letter from Bunny!" Dakota quickly sat down next to me and said "read it, hurry up, open it." Why I didn't tear it open at once I do not know. As Dakota sat in anticipation I looked first at the back and then once again to the front of the envelope. A lump rose in my throat.

Dear mom and dad, I hope you are doing well. I am fine. I miss you both. How is my brother? I never expected to see all the things that Aunt Peggy and Uncle Ian have shown me. They are wonderful people. I am adjusting to school. The kids at first didn't know what to make of a Sioux Indian but they are coming around. I have several friends. Mar, short for Margaret and her brother Rob are two of the best. Aunt Peggy bought me all kinds of school clothes and has already started me in the kitchen of her hotel, when I am not in school. What a wondrous place. I feel like I am in Heaven. The kitchen is large and there are several cooks that cater to every wish of Aunt Peggy. She seems to run the place with an iron hand but I can see why. She never misses a thing. She makes me study and work hard but I love it. Say hi to every one for me. I hope we can come home after school is out. That's what I hope, Uncle Ian talks about it. Love Bunny.

Dakota snatched the letter from my hand and reread it allowed, as I pictured our Raven haired beauty. Dave rubbed his chin but said nothing. Tears ran down Dakota's face as she clutched the letter to her heart.

After a long pause in reflection, I asked "How's Joe and the rest of the family?" "The twins are great, they even fly with me on occasion, that is when I can get them away from their mother. Every one is fine, that is except Joe. Dad, I don't think he will ever get better. In fact I think he is failing." Another lump in my throat and a quick prayer, as I asked, "Such as?" "Well dad I hate to tell you but Joe's balance is gone. He has to use a walker when he has the energy. The rest of the time the doctor has him in a wheelchair." I threw up my hand to get him to stop for a minute, I couldn't take it. Not my Joe, not my big strong Joe. The tears once again welled in my eyes. After a long pause, I got up, went to the stove and poured another cup. This time with a stiff shot of rum. Dakota said nothing. "OK, go on." "Dad, I think you should come home. I have this feeling. I don't want to say it but, well, just come home." He stopped. Dakota started packing our bags. Before long we had the cabin buttoned up. We didn't take the time to service our own plane but started toward Fairbanks with Dave.

Instead of finding Joe at home, we were greeted by a note. The hospital was a cheerless, white and foreboding. Joe lay in a coma, with tubes coming from everywhere and going everywhere. All the kids were with him, but the twins were not allowed in the room. I put my arm around Caroline and wept. Ever the nurse, Dakota held his hand and whispered something in his ear. I sat there with all of them for a while but needed to be alone.

The darkness of the chapel was broken only by the dim light of one candle in a clear red jar, suspended between heaven and earth, by a gold chain. I knelt, dropped my head in my hands and could summon no words. What can a person say at a time like this. Yes I had been in the habit of prayer for a long time. I had contemplated the mysteries of God for ages. Father Paddy, where are you now? Why? What good could come by inflicting this pain on our family? These and seemingly hundreds of other questions flooded through the recesses of my mind, then there was nothing. The room faded away. A long line of people, dressed in all manner of ways, stood before me. I knew instinctively who they were. My family, the rest of the family, the people of old. There were kings and peasants, wealthy and poor. There were old and young, people that I had never met, as well as faces as familiar as my own. One man, small in stature, ragged in appearance, spoke. "Do you know who I am?"

Instinctively, I knew at once. Friar Stefen, the happy wanderer. The old monk my dad told about in his sagas. More astounding were his next words. "We are with you. We are always with you. We are as close as blood. You are one with us just as we are all one with our

God. Death and life are two opposites. We are here to claim your sons life for life. He will not die. Be patient, pray, give thanks, for you will rejoice. Go and tell your family that your son will be healed, have faith that this will be done." With that, all disappeared. The chapel once again bathed in the soft glow of the red candle light.

I sat for a long time in the glow of the candle, at first doubting the things I saw and heard ,then fully believing. I gave thanks. Not just thanks for their words of hope but thanks for all that we had. I left the chapel with thanksgiving in my heart for the family, the long, long, line of people that make up all families.

Joe's wife stayed at his side while the rest of us went home for something to eat. The drive way was packed with cars and pick ups, so packed that we had to park in the hanger. The house bulged with people. The smells of food filled the air as ladies of all ages brought in their best dishes. The house was silent as a tomb, as I brought them up to date on Joe's illness. I could not contain my self any longer. "He will be healed." The looks from the people said that they had doubt. I repeated, "he will be healed."

I had not yet told Dakota of the chapel incident, "Paul, we need to talk." She quietly took me into the bed room and asked, "What was that all about?" "He will be healed Dakota." I then told her of the chapel visit. Dakotas words reinforced my faith. "Paul, when we went into his room and I took his hand I could feel a warm glow from me to him. I whispered to him and told him every thing would be all right." We grabbed a bite to eat and went back to the hospital.

Dakota stayed for a while, then Dave came in. Dave and I sat with him all night. Early the next morning some one else came in. The doctor caught me in the hall as I was leaving and told me in the guarded words of doctors that he did not expect for Joe to live. I told him that I knew that he would. We parted ways as he turned and hurried down the hall, shaking his head.

Joe did not improve. A week past and I began to have doubts. While back in the chapel, I once again had a visit. A welcome visit from an old friend. I did not see him but I knew that he was there with me. Fr Paddy. There was no doubt as I felt his presence and words of consolation within my heart. "Hold firm lad, hold firm."

A long two weeks, led into a longer three weeks. One morning as Dakota and I sat at home having breakfast, the phone rang. "Ladonna, what is happening?" "Hold on dad, Joe is awake. The doctors have pulled out all his tubes. He is sitting up and asking for something to eat." "We'll be right there", as I quickly hung up the phone and grabbed Dakota and half drug her out the door.

There he was, sitting up in bed with both arms wrapped around the twins and a wife with tears of joy streaming down her face. "Hi dad, how the hell are you?" Did I just hear what I heard? His speech rang clear as a bell. "When can I go home dad?"

Chapter 31

Rejoice in the Goodness of the Lord

There remained no reason for Joe to stay in the hospital beyond one more week. The doctors remained dumbfounded. We took him home to continue rehabilitation under the ever watchful eye of Dakota.

The party lasted for two days. We knew that Joe would be fine. It was generally accepted that there must have been a blood clot left over from the crash that finally broke loose and caused the coma. What ever, I for one was the happiest man alive. We stayed around for as long as we were needed. As we packed up our few things, we could hear Ladonna, Dave, and Joe planning his return to the air.

The site of home from the air was especially sweet as Dave glided in for a landing. He made a quick turn around ,we off loaded supplies and once again he took to the air. The harshness of winter was over but it still remained cold. Once inside Dakota waved her arms to produce body heat as I stoked the old stove. It wasn't long before we were as cozy as ever.

After a few days of rest we longed to see Swift Antelope. The dawn of a late winter morning found me in the hanger. I worked most of the morning preparing the Cessna for our trip. Is amazing how many things one must check after laying up an aircraft for most of the winter. The most damage was done by pack rats. They had their treasures stashed here and there through out the plane. Dakota called and I went in for lunch. I handed her three spoons, two forks, and one of her ear rings. "Where in the world did you find my ear ring?" She laughed as I told her of the job that awaited me when I went back to work. " I'll help, I need to get out side." We finished the short afternoon cleaning out the plane and taking a nest out of the engine compartment. "I hate to think of what will be in the Cub when I check it." Dakota's reply, "Perhaps we will find a bracelet that has been missing."

Early morning two days later found me in final preparation for our flight. The cabin of the Cessna packed with our clothes, winter survival gear, food and gifts for the families that we would visit.

One final check of the heated engine ,the prop swung and the engine barked to life. I did a longer warmup than usual just to be on the safe side. I opened the throttle and the aircraft broke loose from the snow. The Cessna lurched as we gained speed. We lifted off as expected at the far end of the strip. Tuk, ever the traveler stuck his head out of Dakota's parka to see the ground disappear behind him.

We took the same route that Dakota had taken on her earlier trip. Occasionally clouds tried to block our way through the many valleys. These were met with simple turns as I managed to avoid the ridges. We crossed over the last pass to see the lights of the village off in the distance. I dropped the Cessna onto the strip and taxied to an area that looked good to tie down. Nothing like a visitor in town to bring out the crowds. Well perhaps not crowds in this case. We were met by Swift Antelope and several friends. You should have seen the look on his face when he found the visitors to be his parents. The steam rose from his breath as he quickly introduced us to his friends. "What are you all doing out here?" I said as I asked Swift Antelope about the spot I picked to park. "We are just riding the machines, just cruising around. You are in a good spot dad." At that, we bedded down the Cessna and with mom hanging on his machine we were off. I rode with a kid that I never saw again.

We had thought that Swift Antelope might stay with Noma the Village Health Aide. Not so, he had found a home with Vern White Wolf and his family. Swift Antelope told me that the two girls at Noma's house drove him up the wall.

Vern insisted we stay at his place. His two sons were grown and on their own. That left one girl about Swift Antelopes age. It wasn't until we got back home that it dawned on me, perhaps that was the reason Swift Antelope wanted to stay with Vern.

Vern's wife was short as expected. She had a personality that reminded me of my mother. She cooked a great meal also. The grub that we brought with us proved to be enough for all of us and then some. I liked these people. Friendly by nature, always joking, always caring about our comfort. At the time I didn't notice how well Swift Antelope and Sarah got along. Vern and I became fast friends and soon were in the planning stage of some future hunt. I asked him how he came to have a flying service and found his story much as my own. Years before some greenhorn from the South stacked his plane on the runway in a storm. The owner wasted no time getting a ride back to Fairbanks and just left the plane. As a kid Vern had wanted to fly. When he saw the opportunity to have a plane, he waited a while. The owner never returned so he took it as his own. Being as resourceful as most Eskimos that I know, he fixed her up. He said that it took months but months was all he had. He taught him self to fly with the help of others just as I had done. To my surprise I found that we were the same age. Vern had his flying service but lacked the money or knowledge to go any further. One night over coffee he said that he wanted a fishing and hunting lodge. One thing led to another and before I knew it I had the basics of a plan.

Dakota took advantage of the opportunity and spent a considerable amount of time helping Noma. Three of the best days of our lives were spent with Vern and his family. The people of the village treated us as their own. Leaving is always the hardest and leaving them all was most difficult. We asked Swift Antelope if he wanted to come home with us but he declined. He said that he liked the kids and the life. He felt that he and Vern still had a lot to accomplish. Dakota and I met his teachers, who all said that he was doing well and fit right in. He was even taking some classes in native studies. Could it be that it was because Vern's daughter was also in the class?

Home loomed close as we glided in. Chores done, the place closed in around us as snug as a good buffalo robe.

I told Dakota of the idea I had while in the village. "Give it a try Paul, what have you got to lose?" I sat at the table pen in hand and back to the stove.

Dear Ian and Peggy. We hope all is well with you. Hope our daughter is behaving well and not too much bother. We are all doing fine, winter is almost over. Well I better get to the point. I know how you have wanted to locate in this area and the difficulty you have had in finding the right spot. I think I have the answer. We met a man from Anaktuvuk village. I have the utmost respect for him and feel that we may be able to have a business partner. As you know, we have been unable to expand our flying service due to the overload of work already on our books. Even with Joe's recent recovery and eventual return to work we would need an additional base of operations, and help. My new friend Vernon White Wolf may fit just such a bill. He knows the area of the Brooks Range we would best operate in, like the palm of his hand. In addition being entitled to operate in that area would be a major asset. Vern has desired to expand also, has a spot picked out for a lodge and the connections to make it happen.

I offer this plan for your consideration. I am able to expand Vern's fleet and lend him the capitol to get started. If you two desire we can enter into a mutual arrangement to build the lodge. I know that Peggy has said more than once that she would like to have her own food operation. A person of her caliber would be a great asset to such a venture. Let us know soon and say hello to Bunny for us. Sincerely, Paul.

On Dave's next supply visit he took the letter with him to post. That done, all we had to do was to sit back and dream of the possibility of a new adventure.

Three weeks later Dave flew in with two passengers. Joe exited the door looking young and fit. I should have been ready but I forgot. Ian slapped me on the back and embraced me in a big bear hug. "How the hell are ye lad?" Choking for breath I reached out my hand to shake only to feel the crush. Will I ever learn?

We wasted no time as the next day, Ian. Joe, and I all boarded the Cessna and were off to the village. We landed at noon and were greeted by Vern, as he worked on his plane. I introduced every one and that evening after a great meal we sat down to business. Vern had no idea of my plan and was taken back at such an offer. Soon he jumped at the chance and plans were made to fly over Vern's chosen site.

The next day we woke to a howling snow storm and we, though disappointed, elected to wait for clear weather. We passed the day in further plans for our future. Drawings of a lodge emerged on yellow paper as each person put in his two cents. Ian wanted twenty rooms,

I wanted ten, Vern only wanted a place to bring his clients and had no idea what size he would choose. Joe thought more of the facilities for the help as well as his own quarters. The three pilots readily agreed on the hanger set up.

The next day broke clear and beautiful. The weather remained perfect as we flew WNW and viewed Chandler Lake for the first time. Though frozen over and white as far as the eye could see we fell in love with it. We flew North and down the Chandler River and followed it for a time as it went on to the Arctic Sea.

We flew ever increasing circles around the lake. The area though barren, revealed sheep in the mountains and other game in the valleys. When Vern pointed to the site he wanted we dropped in on the lake with snow flying off the skies. The site seemed perfect as we sat in the cabin of the plane for a few minutes then took off for the village.

Once again we sat around Vern's table laying plans. Swift Antelope hung on every word and wanted to see the site for himself. Vern told him that he would take him there soon and seemed to settle that. With a hand shake, agreements were made and we left for our cabin above Wiseman.

Vern would head up the flying service in his region and act as guide. In addition he would provide the native manpower for scenic river trips as well as hunting and fishing. Ian would build and manage the lodge, I would put up the money and provide the air craft and linking service to the village where Vern would ferry clients to the lodge. Joe would work with Vern and if he could get his licence back would join the group in the air. We were sure that Peggy would provide the fine meals that we all relished. We stopped at the cabin for a short time and elaborated our plans to Dakota. She then flew Ian and Joe back to Fairbanks.

A new adventure. I had the cabin to myself and could day dream all I wanted of our ideas. It didn't take long to envision Bunny working with Peggy and Swift Antelope working and learning from Vern. By the time Dakota returned a week later, I had it all planned in my head. Dakota and I talked about the plans for hours. She however, felt that I was a little hasty in putting the kids in the picture. "Paul, what makes you think that they will even want to spend their lives in the Arctic as you do?" For a moment she took the wind out of my sails.

"Well sweetie I don't, but I have the feeling that they will jump at the chance. What do you think, can you picture ether one of them , say, living in New York City?"

Spring found Ian fast at work as general contractor on the lodge. We had settled on ten guest rooms, a kitchen designed by Peggy, staff quarters, as well as everything else needed for such a venture. While Ian labored on the logistics of such an operation, I took Vern to Anchorage to pick up the first of two planned Otter Aircraft. While Vern took training in the Otter, I took in the sights. Though the sights around Anchorage and the Keni Peninsula are great, I soon tired of them and returned to work with Vern, as he finished training. We took delivery on the first Otter and took off from Merrell field in a thick fog. As we flew over Cook Inlet the fog lifted and the small mountain called Sleeping Lady came into view. Vern flew ahead of me and about 1000 feet higher. We had planned on following the Highway from Talkeetna to Fairbanks but when Mt Denali came into view in all its glory, we veered off course , for a closer look. At over 20,000 feet the great mountain stands heads above all its sisters. Since we had used up too much fuel we returned to Talkeetna, landed, had lunch, then returned to the air. We resumed our flight plan and landed at my strip in Fairbanks in the early spring evening. Vern went on ahead and flew his new Otter on to the village. I spent a few days with the kids then returned home.

I was shocked to see Bunny run out the door of the cabin as I swung the Cessna around and cut the engine. Before I could get out of the seat she opened the door and climbed in, giving me a big kiss. "Dad, I love you."

What a reunion. Bunny talked a blue streak, trying to get all the months of her absents said in two breaths. She went on and on about her school, her friends, life in Scotland and Aunt Peggy. When Dakota got up to prepare supper, Bunny would have none of it. She talked a blue streak all the while preparing dishes she had learned from her mentor. Now Dakota is a good cook but you have to only lift your nose in the direction of Bunny's stove, to realize fine cooking.

I ate so much I could hardly lift myself from the table. Bunny dragged me back. "Hold on dad, one more thing," as she laid a Scottish dessert in front of me.

Aunt Peggy wanted to be with Ian so much that she reigned her position early, took Bunny out of school and caught a plane for Alaska. I asked Bunny if it would hurt her grades and she said that it didn't matter as she was going to work with Aunt Peggy. I looked at Dakota and gave her a wink as in, "I told you so."

Chapter 32

The Lodge on Hallowed Ground

As part of the deal, I needed to be at the building site from time to time. I found the building "boom" in full swing as I landed on the make shift strip at the edge of the lake. Vern had floats already on the Otter as I saw it from the air. We were set up for both float and tundra tires at the site. I found the hangar facilities already in their final stages of finish. What an expensive operation I thought as I taxied up.

The booming voice of Ian could be heard shouting orders to the builders. I wondered if he had ever been a Sargent Major. He certainly had the voice for one. Before I could make my presence noticed I could hear the roar of a converted C119 military cargo aircraft on final. How in the world will he land on this short strip I thought.

It seemed as tho the pilot had reversed the props almost before he hit the strip. Full flaps down, brakes howling and dust flying, the giant plane stopped just short of the end and swung around.

Once again the site lay quiet as the Load master took care of the cargo. How in the word could all that equipment get packed in that plane?

As I walked to the future lodge, Swift Antelope came from behind and scared the crap out of me with one of his pranks. I grabbed him in a mock head scrub and then a bear hug. "Dad, I'm glad you're here, Vern and I are planning a hunt. Want to come along?" I still had to find that booming voice, so deferred my answer to a later time.

I became caught up in watching the roof rafters going up as I met a surprise from behind. A giant slap on the back and a grand "how the hell are ye lad." I pitched forward feeling the very life going out of me.

Once again Ian out foxed me. Some day friend, some day I'll get you back.

The bunk house finished, we ate a great meal by the hired cook. We all sat at a long table supported by saw horses. Rough and tough workmen from seemingly every state voiced rousing conversation. Ian introduced me to the workmen as some big butter and egg man from the East. I had to correct him at once. I told them of my small part in the project as they went back to their conversations obviously not caring a hoot as to who I was. Alright by me.

I was awakened early the next morning by Swift Antelope. "Come on dad, Vern's waiting." I looked at my pocket watch, three AM. "Come on dad get up, I've got the gear, lets go."

Vern had the Otter at full throttle as we came up on the step. The next thing I felt was the Otter lift off the water. We banked a full 360 degrees, as I saw the workmen, one by one heading for breakfast.

We flew North under clear sky's. The river glistened under the early morning sun. Time after time we flew low over broken herds of caribou. Occasionally a bear and even more rare an arctic fox or two. The Tundra stretched for miles in an unbroken chain, devoid of the stamp of man. Small ponds and lakes, shimmered in the Arctic Summer, awaiting the coming of another freeze.

Vern cut the throttle and glided onto one lake sending plumes of cold water flying behind. He cut the engine, as we drifted. Vern called out "get out the fishing gear."

"I thought we were to hunt on this trip" I said, as Swift Antelope deftly flicked a rod tip toward an unseen target. "We are", came from both, "were hunting fish." I had my hopes on a good hunt with rifle and said so. Vern informed me that he had to check out this lake for future clients. I supposed that was good business sense and soon forgot about hunting with rifle. I landed a nice ten pounder as Swift Antelope and Vern both brought in twelve and fourteen pounders, at the same time. After fishing for a short time we had about fifty or sixty pounds of fine cold water fish. We sat on the floats and paddled to shore. In no time Vern and Swift Antelope had a good fire going and the smell of fish in the pan, dispelled all thought of hunting in any other manner.

Swift Antelope filled my cup as I filled my plate. Vern had his first helping finished before I even started. I marveled at all the activities that Swift Antelope had mastered. Vern had done a fine job of teaching this young warrior.

"I think we will add this lake to our schedule," Vern said. He added that he thought we should not over fish it. I liked his conservation methods. Too much of the Arctic is being wasted at the hands of sport and big company profit.

We took turns rekindling a small brushwood fire as each in turn swapped tales. I asked Vern about my last crash, how he came to be in that area and if he saw any dogs. "Nope, I don't recall picking you up and I don't recall any dogs." I rubbed my chin and told him that my son said that he did pick me up. "Nope, ain't me and I'm not getting that old, sure would recall if I did. When did that happen?" I continued my story of the rescue and the date as best as I could remember. Vern thought for a long while, mentally counting on his fingers. "That's strange, I went down to the strip to do some work on my plane long about then. Found my plane came up missing. Now you just don't go missing something as big as an airplane. Strange thing though, I swung around in my tracks looking for my plane and suddenly there it was setting right in front of me. Off in the distance walked two people, a man and a woman best I can recall, one wrapped in a red blanket."

Swift Antelope looked at me and I in turn looked at him, we both smiled. By the time I finished telling some of the story about Rachael and Paul, Vern was scratching his head. The look on his face, said that he didn't believe a word of it.

About the time Swift Antelope picked up a peace of wood and tossed it on the fire we heard a long mournful howl. About two seconds later two people, dressed in buck skins, one with a red blanket, sat cross legged before the fire. Vern fell off the rock he had been sitting on.

By the time he got up, Paul was speaking. "I love a good fire, kind of reminds me of," Vern passed out. When he woke up, Paul continued where he had left off. "Kind of reminds me of the old days. This was our way of life, We sat for hours in our lodge, stoking the fire and telling tales. This is fun, isn't it Vern?"

I have never seen any one so wide eyed or pale as Vern. Thoughts of spirit stories told by his elders must have been crossing his mind.

Paul went on, as Rachael asked if we had any tea. "We used to sit around the lodge fire all winter. That is unless we needed to hunt. Most of the time though, we just sat around telling spirit stories and making arrow heads." Vern's hand shook as he poured hot water over some tea leaves in Rachael's cup. By the time he did the same for Paul he was shaking so badly that he spilled most of it. "That's alright Vern," Rachael said as she offered to pour Paul's cup.

Vern finally recovered enough to listen, as Paul went on. "This tea is good but not like the tea my mother poured for my father. Now that was good tea, it came straight from India, all the way around the Cape of Good Hope."

"You know Vern, one of my ancestors met your ancient people years ago. They were crossing the ice far to the North in the dead of winter. They would have preferred to stay in the warmth of their Igloos but they needed more food. The hunting was not good so they decided to move. They packed up all their belongings and set out to the East." Sparks drifted into the air as Paul threw another piece of wood on the fire. As he was about to continue four more people suddenly appeared. All of them were dressed in old ragged furs. One was much taller and had a complexion unlike the others. Being accustomed to such appearances by spirits, I felt no surprise. This time Swift Antelopes eyes widened as Vernon jumped up in shock.

"Vernon White Wolf, I am Ewotok, brother to your grand fathers of ancient times. Paul and Paul Rachael would know me as Ewotok of the Fish. This is my daughter Ootah and my mother. The tall man is John."

We heard another howl and in that instant Spirit and Broken Eye nuzzled up against Rachael. The circle got so crowded that we all moved back a few feet as I laid on more fire wood. This was getting interesting to say the least. There were so many people that we had to share cups as Swift Antelope and Rachael filled them with hot tea. Ewotok smacked his lips and said that it was good. The old woman withdrew a small flat drum stretched over what appeared to be an ivory hoop.

The old woman started to beat the drum slowly with a piece of bone, as the old man Ewotok went on. "We approve of the site for your lodge Vernon, very good. Our people have camped on that lake for centuries. Many hunts for caribou took place and our people used to trade with people of the South at that place. If you search the far side of the lake you will find markings made by your ancestors on the rocks." I couldn't help but make a mental note for Al to check it out.

The drum stopped, much as it did at the story telling at Point Hope. Cups were filled once again as Rachael and Swift Antelope served up plates of fresh fish. The old man seemed to relish the fish as he wiped his mouth with his sleeve and pronounced "good."

The story resumed as the drum repeated its hypnotic sound. This time it was John that directed the story toward Paul and myself.

"Well both of you, I am glad we finally meet. The line is long. We are all proud of you. We have been watching you and your family for many years. Your family will go on and on into the future. Have no worry.

I had no need to hear these words as I thought of all the people before me and longed to know their stories in more detail. The drum continued as Ewotok resumed. "Vernon we are also proud of you and you will prosper along with Paul Rachael. We want you to know that your," before he could complete his words all vanished.

The camp took on a lonely silence. None of us spoke for a long time. The fire died down and all that remained of it, took a thin trail of smoke to the heavens.

I had often wondered while reading my fathers manuscript what these people looked like. I couldn't wait to tell Dakota and the kids of this latest encounter. Vern spoke first. "What am I going to tell my wife, my people, they will never believe me." Swift Antelope nodded in agreement as I said, "Oh, I think they will."

The first person to meet us when we returned to the lodge was Ian. He was about to give me the "greeting," as I began to call it. I dodged just in time. Dam, I was starting to learn.

I grabbed his arm, "We need to talk my friend," I said, as the four of us headed toward the mess hall. We sat in one corner, out of ear shot of the workers as one by one we related the tale. I thought Ian would be skeptical but he wasn't. We laid plans to search the far side of the lake the next morning.

The next morning Ian gave orders to the foreman as the rest of us ate in silence. After breakfast, we packed enough food for the day and took off on a swift walk. The distance was not far and knowing the general area of our search, not difficult. While we walked we had hopes that the workmen would not notice our destination.

It was as though we were guided by our spirits as we quietly approached the site. There, ten feet up on a rock wall, Petroglyphs, Paintings of many descriptions. The story book of our people. We stood in silence, each man, first looking, than touching our past. This site belonged to us. We were a direct link.

As I looked over the wall, I could see plainly, pictures drawn in ancient fashion, caribou, muskox, wolves, fish, and other smaller creatures of the Arctic. Many hand prints and star appearing pictures, some faded, overgrown with lichens and some as plain as day. This wall told the story of our ancient past. One picture that stood out depicted a hunter, spear in hand, with arm drawn back, about to kill his prey. We all touched this one at once. At that point we made a pact that this site would not be turned over to the university. This belonged to our family.

We sat among the rocks listening to the small waves breaking on the shore. Hammers could plainly be heard across the small lake. Here and there a workman blurted out a bit of profanity, most likely hitting his finger with a hammer.

As the others started in on the lunch prepared by the camp cook, I looked around. The rocks laying at our feet were mostly of broken shale. Here and there a round moss covered rock. An object unlike the others caught my eye. As I bent to pick it up, I could see the outline of an Ulu, a cutting tool. Made of Ivory, it was of the usual shape. It had a half round blade of Ivory and a handle apparently made of Walrus. I at once thought of Bunny. How fitting for a Native American Chef.

As I ate my lunch the others looked the site over as well. Swift Antelope found several arrow heads laying in plain sight. Ian found a partial bowl. Vernon found the remains of an oil lamp several feet beyond the only bolder in the area.

Chapter 33

Celebration of The People

The lodge was due to be opened on Oct 28th. Joe had a few guests lined up for sight seeing trips in the area. There were a few guests already making reservations for the future. The schedule was not full but enough to tell us that we would be a success.

The week before, family started to arrive. Vernon ferried passengers from the village and Dave brought in friends and family from all over. This was going to be one big shindig.

More light aircraft came in one by one. Swift Antelope and Joe helped unload and as fast as this happened, they were off for another group. People from Fortuna Ledge, Point Hope, Fairbanks, Arctic Village, Anaktuvuk Village and many other points. Some even came by snow machine and two by dog sled.

I had the honor of escorting Ben Bear Hunter as well as two cousins to the lodge. Dakota took over, settling the old man into a comfortable place next to the mammoth stone fireplace. I quickly returned to the strip helping folks with sleeping bags and other gear. I enjoyed our new four wheelers. We had brought up three of them. Ian had one of the carpenters build a trailer large enough for baggage. This we had piled high with every thing from the sleeping bags to sacks and boxes, of many sizes. White Wolf Aviation must have brought most of the village in more hops than I could count.

As I ferried the load of baggage in the trailer to the lodge, The people walked in single file, their breath sending clouds of vapor into the early winter air. Swift Antelope brought up the rear with one of the snow machines. I noticed Sarah holding on tight even though he was only doing two miles per hour.

Peggy had been at the lodge for some time. After my last load from the strip I sat at the end of her kitchen work table, just drinking coffee and watching her work. God was she good looking. I dropped this thought, as Dakota came in. "Paul, we've got tons of guests and I think you need to help me!" My intentions were good with Peggy, just always thought her a good looking woman. I hoped that Dakota couldn't read my thoughts.

There were people everywhere, all talking at the same time. I made the rounds of the large great room introducing myself and asking each person if they had found a place to sleep. Apparently Dakota and Ladonna were way ahead of me. I settled in to getting acquainted with folks.

Ben Bear Hunter sat telling stories to the children. Speaking of children, there must have been thirty or more of them. They came in all shapes and sizes. My twin grand kids were right in the middle of them, lapping up some story that Ben laid before them. Over in the corner next to a glassed in cabinet, sat some one I hadn't noticed before. As I approached he stopped talking to the short dark skin man next to him and stuck his hand out. "Father Francis Iluak, you must be Paul?" "Yes Father, I don't believe we've met before." Father Francis quickly introduced his companion. "Paul this man is Ralph Ataninnuaq. Ralph is a Deacon." Both men were short and obviously Inuit. Ralph gave a warm vigorous hand shake, additionally placing his left hand over mine. Father Francis interjected that they were new friends of Ladonna and Al.

Just then Dakota called me to one more of her many tasks. "Excuse me duty calls." Father Francis and Ralph sat back down as I went off to see what Dakota wanted. On the way I caught a glimpse of two teen age figures in a deep embrace. They quickly parted at my passing. Strange I thought, that looked like Swift Antelope and Sarah.

The people of Fairbanks and the people of Point Hope mingled in conversation. The people of Anaktuvuk Village met with the people of Arctic Village. In between, this one held conversation with that one.

"Supper", Bunny called as the dinner bell rang. The people scrambled to the long tables laden with mounds of food of every description. I had thought that we had a crowd in the great room until I saw the number of women exiting the kitchen with more food.

All the children sat at one table supervised by several women that I thought I knew but couldn't place. Ian called for the blessing. "Father Francis, will you do the honors?"

Father Francis began with the sign of the cross, I noticed that some of the people didn't seem to know what to make of the gesture. Father Francis then went on. He thanked the cooks for the wonderful food, the owners for the lodging and then Our Father in Heaven for all that we had. He blessed the food and the people than gave a hearty amen.

Wave after wave of bowls, dishes, platters, and baskets passed round the tables. Beaver, ptarmigan, moose, seal, walrus, arctic char, salmon, blueberries, kale, turkey, yams, mashed potatoes, There must have been eight or ten types of bread, I lost count as I passed up on some of the items. With my plate filled to the brim, I saw Ian as he went for seconds. The people ate until they groaned. The sounds of merriment mixed with the over full bellies of the men rounded out the meal.

Talk went late into the night. The children one by one were put to bed. The women, finished in the kitchen, joined the men. There were not enough chairs, so people sat in a large circle. Swift Antelope, ever the fire bug, fed the fireplace. Ben Bear Hunter told stories as some one from Arctic Village beat a drum in time to the tales. One by one people drifted off to their rooms.

The next morning found Tuk and I setting in the large kitchen, I, holding my head and Tuk sniffing at something that Peggy handed him. "How do you do it Peggy?" "Do what Paul?" " manage all the food and seemingly with out the slightest effort." Dakota came in and sat with us. Peggy continued, "well Paul it's not hard at all. I think I was born to it, just as Bunny is." I looked over as Bunny came in and caught Aunt Peggy's last words. "In to what Aunt Peggy?" "Your Dad just asked how we did it, how we could put such a meal together." Bunny said, "that's easy dad, we were born into it."

I excused myself for a minute and went to my room. I pulled the forgotten Ulu from my pocket and took it back to the kitchen. "I held out my hand and said,"here Bunny." I handed her the Ulu, expecting a question from her. "Do you know what it is?" "Of course dad, it's an Ulu." She turned it over several times admiring the patina of it's age and the craftsmanship. I told her where it came from and what I knew about it, as she put it in a safe place, gave me a big hug and went back to preparing breakfast. By this time I started to feel unwelcome as more women came into the kitchen. I could see why Peggy thought it easy to put on a big meal. Every woman seemed to know exactly what had to be done and when. As I left, Bunny was proudly showing the women the ancient Ulu.

Not counting the children, Ian and I thought that we must have about sixty or seventy guests. The day had been planned for days. Swift Antelope had a trail groomed in the snow, suitable for people to walk. The trail went from the lodge, and around the lake, as the lake had open places in it. We made arrangements for Father Francis to say Mass. Swift Antelope already had a table for an alter and planned to take some of the old people in the baggage trailer ahead of us.

After another big meal, all the people walked to the site. Vernon White wolf led the pilgrimage. The noon day light penetrated the surroundings with dark, almost imperceptible shadows. Steam rose from the breath of the long line of people. The temperature lay at nineteen degrees, with no wind. The only sounds came from footsteps crunching on the frozen surface of the trail.

As the people arrived, they circled around the makeshift alter. Fr Francis took off his parka and quickly put on the vestments. I thought him to be rather brave, as with Tuk peeking out of my parka I was still cold. Deacon Ralph lit the alter candles. I could see the people gazing at the marvelous petroglyphs, as candle light played ghostly shadows across them. Father Francis wasted no time in beginning. "In the name of the Father and of the Son and of the Holy Spirit. Brothers and sisters we are gathered in this hallowed place to celebrate Our Lord and to dedicate this site to the memory of our ancestors." My mind wandered over the centuries, John and Ootah, Ewotok of the fish, The long line of my family branching from these people of the Arctic. Here we were, Scott, Lakota, Swede, Inuit, and any number of other peoples banded together to celebrate our being, with the one who makes all being possible.

I could feel the presence of our ancient ones and as my mind once again drifted back to the present, Deacon Ralph finished the readings. Father Francis spoke the Gospel, then the Sermon. I once again slipped from reality, flying over Arctic spaces. Turns flew with ravens, eagles flew with swallows. Whales swam with seals and wolves lay with the mountain sheep. Peoples from every corner of the Arctic gathered in one great council. At the center stood a man in white, his being dazzled like the sun as the night shown with galaxies of stars. The Aurora Borealis plunged waterfalls of color across the frozen land. The people began to dance in ever widening then narrowing circles, drums beat the hypnotic rhythm of the North.

I once again returned to reality as Dakota gently nudged me forward and whispered that I was holding up the Communion line. I let her go ahead of me, as one by one the people of God received the Eucharist.

After the Mass Father Francis took the incense burner from the hand of The Deacon. He sent wave after wave of incense up the wall and onward to Heaven all the while chanting prayers of the people. With that the long line with Swift Antelope in the lead returned to the lodge.

Father Francis sat next to the roaring fire. Next to him Ben Bear Hunter chatted with the Deacon. Steaming cups of coffee were passed around as Bunny and some of the other ladies carried the pots. Thawing parkas sat in a heap on the floor as some of the children had a free for all in the middle of the pile. Tuk peeked his head out of the pile just as one of the children landed almost on top of him. My eye ran around the room, taking in the merriment. Over in the corner, just behind the grandfather clock stood two young people obviously entwined in loves embrace. Heck, that young man was Swift Antelope. I got up to check this out, only to be met by Dakota, who needed something done. By the time I got back the two kids were gone. I sat the incident aside for the time being.

I felt fortunate to sit next to Father Francis at supper. "What do you think father? I mean what is your impression of the day?" "Paul, I think that this was a fantastic day. You know these people are mine also. I mean not just as their priest but by blood. I think this site will be a great source of pride for all of us. I hope that it is never forgotten."

Epilogue

By
Ladonna Rachael McAuffe

The time following the great dedication at the lake was a happy time for all of us. Al and I and the twins stayed at the lodge long enough to see it open. Most of the people that were there for the dedication trickled away over the next several days. Father Francis and dad had long talks at the fireside in the great room. I would have liked to be a bug on the wall and listen in but I guess it's better this way.

In the closing hours of the dedication days, there were long story telling sessions. Ben Bear Hunter, dad, Vernon White Wolf, and several others took turns telling tales late into each night. I thought Ben Bear Hunter, who I suppose is my Great Uncle or perhaps my Great, Great Uncle kept the children captivated by his tales of young children, of days long past. Dad told tales of the family from my grand father's manuscript of "Skipping Rock". There were hunts, feasts, wars and weddings which kept the older people enthralled.

Bunny and Peggy worked long hours to make sure all were fed. I don't think any one went away hungry, I know I didn't. Joe, my brother, announced the impending birth of a new child. Swift Antelope worked long and hard servicing the aircraft of White Wolf Aviation, as well as those picking up passengers on their way home.

Dad and Dakota went back to the cabin but soon became restless. They closed up the cabin and came here to Fairbanks. Dad announced his intention to make a trip Outside. This came as a shock to us as he had never given a hint that he had any interest in doing so. None the less, The two of them made reservations and flew South.

We never thought that we would see the day that Paul Rachael McAuffe would leave Alaska. From time to time we received letters and cards from all over the lower forty eight. After about three months they returned. I had never seen dad with a tan. He was as dark as could be.

It was nice to have them back. I had really never been too far from his wisdom and love before and I missed him. I missed Dakota also, I could not wait to give her a big hug.

They shared stories of their trip and of course pictures. They had visited the old home county of dad's grand father, Jacob McAuffe. I knew of him from dads book and was surprised to hear that dad had a lot of information about his life after he left Nome.

Not one to stay in one place too long, dad and Dakota returned to the cabin. We did not see them again until Swift Antelope's wedding. Dad was fit to be tied and said so. "How can he do this, he's too young." Dad went on and on until Dakota managed to calm him down in her usual sweet way. "Now Paul, you know that you were married the first time when you were about the same age." That fixed him. After that he warmed to the idea after spending some time at the lodge and getting to know Sarah. When I met Sarah, my heart melted. She has beautiful dark eyes, Raven black hair down to her shoulders, much as Bunny's was before she cut it. Sarah has a sweet disposition. Dakota loves her to pieces and she won dad over immediately.

The wedding was held at the lodge with Deacon Ralph officiating. Ian stood in as best man and Bunny as the bridesmaid. Dinner of course, was done by Peggy.

Both of the kids worked at the lodge. Wedding gifts helped with furnishing their cozy little cabin. Dad gave Swift Antelope the knife of his grand father Charlie Two Bears. To our surprise he gave Swift Antelope his Cub. No one ever thought that he would part with it.

Dakota gave Sarah the big bear skin rug that she had received from Ben Bear Hunter. Once again I couldn't believe that they would part with these precious gifts.

With the wedding celebration over, Joe flew his family and Dave back to Fairbanks and we followed in my Beaver. Dad and Dakota said good bye to the kids and left for the cabin.

Not only were we surprised by my fathers actions, at giving the Cub and the other items away but they still had something up their sleeve.

About a month later dad and Dakota visited Fairbanks once more. We all sat around the table after dinner. The way dad fidgeted I could tell that he had some kind of plan. Al, Dave, Joe and the rest of us listened intently as Dakota said, "Well Paul are you going to tell them or am I?"

"I will dear, give me a minute to put my thoughts together." He went on, " For a long time I have thought about the remoteness of living at the old cabin. I have never felt good since they put in that dam haul road and pipeline so close. I feel like I'm dam well living in the city. I know it's quite a few miles away but I'll swear I can hear the dam trucks on a clear night."

We continued to be all ears as dad fumbled around and pulled out some papers. "Dakota and I have talked about this for a long time." He fidgeted some more then went on. "The old cabin has been in continual use since the 1920s. Its still warm and cosy but badly in need of something. I want to tear it down. I don't think any of you would want to live there." I think all of us spoke the same thing at the same time. "How can you even think of doing that, it's been your life?" Joe added, dad, we have all been attached to that place for our whole lives, it doesn't seem right to think that way. Dave had about the same opinion. I did not think it a very wise idea and said so. Dad said, "well, lets put that thought aside for a few minutes and go on."

Dakota got up from the table and poured another round of coffee. Dad continued. "We have also decided to give up our share of McAuffe Aviation. These papers give each of you kids an equal share of our end of the business." He tilted his chair back, then just as suddenly tipped his chair forward again, shuffled some more papers and went on. "Ladonna and Al, this gives you two the house and one acre, not including the hanger. That remains with the business. Joe and Dave, these checks are the equivalent of the value of the house."

Dad had just given up every thing that he owned in Fairbanks. The boys and I sat there looking at one another dumbfounded. The only question that we could ask. Why?

"Dakota and I want to build a new place at the lodge. I no longer have any need or desire to have a hand in the aviation business. You all know that I have stayed out of it for some time. We have enough cash and other investments to last the rest of our lives. Not only that, we have an interest in the lodge as well as White Wolf Aviation. I want more time to write. The manuscript that I just finished is really finished and I am asking you Ladonna to write the epilogue to it and get it published. The proceeds can go to all the grand children when we are gone. Besides that, you all are adults. We want to be near Swift

Antelope and Bunny. Vernon and his wife are dear friends and we love Ian and Peggy as much as we love you. In addition, we enjoy the remoteness of the lodge.

Dad burned the old cabin in a simple ceremony. We set grave stones in memory of Noah and Dorthy next to a newer cabin. Dad allowed that perhaps we would want to return there from time to time.

I asked dad one day, about our spirit visitors. He said, "Well Ladonna, they are God's messengers in a form that we can recognize." I still wonder to this day.

Their new home sets a short distance from the lodge. It is built solidly of log and rock. The red blanket lays neatly folded at the foot of their bed. Sarah thought the big bear rug fit better in front of the fire place. Swift Antelope hung the knife of Charlie Two bears over the mantle. The Bow with Arrows, that Paul made for dad, hangs next to it, along with the old skin bag containing the Skipping Rock. Buried in the hearth, covered with a large removable stone, lays the old tin box containing the remainder of our treasures of the past. Carved within the face of the mantle are the words, "Peace be with you."